HER COWBOY'S
TRIPLETS

SASHA SUMMERS

MIX
Paper from
responsible sources

FSC
FSC C007454

This book is produced from independently certified FSC™
paper to ensure responsible forest management.

For more information visit: www.harpercollins.co.uk/green

Printed and bound in Spain
by CPI, Barcelona

MILLS & BOON

First Published in Great Britain 2018
by Mills & Boon, an imprint of HarperCollins*Publishers*
1 London Bridge Street, London, SE1 9GF

Her Cowboy's Triplets © 2018 Sasha Best

ISBN: 978-0-263-26499-9

38-0518

For Suellen Foxhall.

Your love of life and joyful spirit
were gifts to all who knew you.

Chapter One

India Boone pushed her glasses into place and shoved another pencil into the top-knot of curls atop her head. "Work. Please work." She typed in the code again, pressed Enter and held her breath. The same error box popped up on the computer screen. India covered her face with her hands and bit back a string of curses.

"Mom?" her five-year-old son, Cal, and his dog, Tanner, peered over the edge of the desk. "How many years before the Indians got here did the dinosaurs go extinct? Was it fifty-five or sixty-five millions years?"

She grinned at them, her frustration momentarily forgotten. How could she stay frustrated in the face of such adorableness? Most five-year-olds wouldn't think about these things, but Cal was anything but normal. He was gifted and talented—something his old private school in Dallas was thrilled about. According to them, he was very gifted. Not that she'd needed anyone to tell her that.

"I'm not sure Cal. A long, *long* time. But if you want a firm answer we can go to the fort later on and ask Ada." If the internet was working, she could answer the question in no time. But that was the problem. Her computer skills were solid—once internet service was set up. She skimmed the software manual again, hoping she'd missed something.

"Ada knows everything about Fort Kyle, doesn't she?" Cal asked.

"Pretty much." India nodded. "Too bad she doesn't know everything about installing software."

"Take a break? Maybe it'll come to you after?" Cal suggested.

She smiled at him, rubbed behind Tanner's soft ear and took off her glasses, tucking them into their case. "A break, huh?" she asked, tugging the pencils free from her hair and rubbing the back of her head.

"Sara said the Soda Shop is almost out of peach ice cream for the year," Cal said, grinning. "That's your favorite, isn't it?"

"You know it is." And it sounded delicious.

He stood, tucking his favorite plesiosaur dinosaur into his pocket. "Let's go get some. Come on, Mom, you deserve it."

"You're allergic to peaches. What about you?" she asked, knowing exactly what he wanted. Something chocolate. Cal was all about the chocolate.

"Yeah, but…" He hooked his thumbs in his belt loops, rocking on his boots. "I'm not allergic to chocolate. Or ice cream. Or brownies."

Tanner stood, tail wagging, his golden gaze bouncing between them. The Belgian Malinois came around, pushing his broad head under her hand and leaning into her until she scratched behind his floppy, dark ear.

"See, even Tanner needs a break," he tacked on.

She giggled, loving the smile on her son's face. "You're willing to suffer through a brownie sundae for me?"

"Sure." He laughed. "You *did* work at the school lots this week. Now you're helping Gramma and Papa."

That was her—a jack-of-all-trades. Finding steady, good-paying work in a town the size of Fort Kyle was near impossible. Instead, she took what she could. Including installing internet and new inventory and accounting software for her parents' antiques shop, along with substitute teaching and filling in at her parents' dude ranch when they were shorthanded.

"It's the weekend, Mom," Cal added.

She'd come into the shop on her Sunday afternoon because it was closed. Meaning her father wasn't around to stop her from dragging their business into the twenty-first century. His insistence on using paper ledgers and calculators took twice as long, and other than being inefficient and exhausting, the system was prone to errors. Her father would use the computer's noncooperation as proof that relying on a "box full of wires" was "the stupidest idea" she'd ever had.

"A break it is." She pushed out of the wobbly office chair and flipped off the office lamp. If nothing else, Cal's patience deserved ice cream.

Cal led her to the front door of the antiques shop, Tanner trailing after them. "Did you know Gramma brought over another box of stuff from the big house?" He held the door open for her.

"She did?" She pulled the shop door shut and locked it. "I haven't seen it or inventoried anything new."

"And Papa snuck in two more when Gramma was talking to that loud lady from Nebraska." He grinned up at her. "Hope Gramma doesn't notice anything missing this time."

"Let's hope not."

There was no denying her parents had too many things. Her mother's penchant for collecting bordered on hoarding. The ranch house attic was packed tight, the closets were overflowing and their storage shed was a virtual museum of unique and fascinating items. Items her mother treasured. Items her father was determined to sell and make a tidy profit from.

When he'd tried to sneak things from the house into the shop, he'd gotten caught. Her mother hadn't talked to her father for two days, which was torture for him. Woodrow Boone had one weakness: his wife. Apologies, flowers and chocolates, whatever made her happy, he did it.

But Woodrow Boone also never gave up—the man had a stubborn streak a mile wide. Within a few weeks, he'd managed the feat again, but this time he was smart enough to pick things from buried trunks and the back of closets. So far her mother had yet to miss any of it.

Her parents' relationship was a mystery to her, but it had lasted for thirty-six years. Her marriage had barely lasted three years. Her divorce had left wounds so deep there was still some healing to do.

"Sky is pink." Cal pointed at the horizon. A pink sunset and wafer-thin clouds greeted the eye. The West Texas breeze held the promise of fall. She leaned against the wood railing, letting the familiar sights and sounds of the small town ease the stress from her shoulders. The town was proof positive that the Old West wasn't just the stuff of John Wayne movies. She and Cal were living it.

For a few more months.

"Pretty, isn't it?" he asked.

"It is." She lingered, appreciating the rugged beauty of the place where she'd grown up. When she'd been in Dallas, she'd missed Fort Kyle. Missed her sweet sister, Scarlett, and her mother's smile. But now that she was here, she was reminded of the reason she left every time she looked at her father. He wore his disappointment for everyone to see. Failed marriage, flunked out of school and a son who was more interested in books than ranching—she was an all-around embarrassment to the Boone name. She'd come home because she wouldn't let her pride keep Cal hungry. She shoved thoughts of her past and her father aside and opened the door of the Soda Shop for her son. "Ready for the Monarch Festival? And the cattle drive?"

Cal nodded. "Think Papa will let me ride a real horse? On my own?"

India wrinkled her nose. "We'll see, Cal." But she knew the answer. Her father wouldn't spend the time teaching his grandson how to ride, even though it was tradition for Boone men. Cal hadn't grown up on the ranch. He'd grown up in Dallas, a city boy with little time in the saddle. Like her ex-husband.

Cal's father always said Fort Kyle was too remote and too backwater for a man like him. But India knew the truth. He'd never been welcome in her hometown. She'd met Jim Thomas Cleburne—JT to his friends—while away at college and had gotten so swept up in their relationship, she'd eventually dropped out of school. Marrying into the wealthy Boone family had suited JT just fine, but not her father. Woodrow Boone pegged JT as bad news from the first time she'd brought him home to the ranch on a school holiday, and he'd done his best to drive the man away while they were dating. India had been too outraged by her father's meddling and harsh treatment of JT to consider he might be right.

As a self-described man of high ideals, JT liked the *idea* of success—but not the work. A pattern developed. JT chased after the latest get-rich scheme to wealth only to take his disappointment out on her when it all fell apart—and she had the scars to prove it. When he'd finally left, she'd been physically bruised and emotionally damaged, with a pile of debt and a vague assurance that he'd found a sure thing.

That was three years ago. Three years with no letters, phone calls or birthday or Christmas cards, which suited India just fine.

India and her son each took a seat on the bar stools lining the service counter.

"Hey, Cal. Hey, Miss India. What'll it be?" Sara asked from her spot behind the counter.

Cal grinned at the teenager, the shop's namesake. "You don't know?"

She tapped her chin with a finger. "Let me think. Hmm, a hot-fudge brownie sundae?" she asked, smiling. "And some water for Tanner?"

Tanner's ear perked up at his name, but he stayed seated at India's feet—on his best behavior.

Cal nodded, tipping his straw cowboy hat back. "Yes, ma'am."

"Hats off inside, Cal," India whispered, pleased when he did as she said.

"What would you like, Miss India?" Sara asked.

"A single scoop of peach ice cream in a sugar cone." Brody Wallace's voice rang out, the slight gravel a pleasant surprise. He was the last person she'd expected to find sitting on the bar stool beside Cal. But there he was, all tawny eyes and red-gold hair, broad shoulders—broader and bigger than she remembered. But then, it had been years since she'd seen him last. "If I remember correctly?" He grinned, his brows rising in question.

India stared at him, stunned. By his transformation. And his presence. It was so good to see him. "Brody?" She hopped off her stool, hesitating seconds before wrapping her arms around his neck. "It's so good to see you. It's been too long. When did you get back in town? You visiting? Is your dad okay?"

He pulled back, his eyes crinkling from his grin.

"Hold on, now. I'll pick one. My dad's fine. Ornery as ever, but fine." His gaze explored her face, his smile never wavering. "You look good, Goldilocks."

His nickname for her made her hug him again. Brody Wallace had been her very best friend in the world. Having the comfort of his arms around her now reminded her just how much she'd missed him. He'd been her shoulder through thick and thin, her confidant and her adviser. The last few years, when things had been so damn hard, she'd thought about reaching out to him. But calling him after all this time had seemed wrong—selfish.

"You okay?" he whispered.

She nodded, forcing herself to step back. "It's just so good to see you."

His eyes narrowed just a hint, stared a little too hard. "You, too."

"Mom?" India felt Cal's tug on her arm. *"Goldilocks?"*

She stepped back then, sliding an arm around her son. "Cal, this is Brody. He was my best friend growing up here." She squeezed her son's shoulder. "Brody, this is my son, Cal."

Brody held his hand out. "Nice to meet you, Cal. And who's this?" he asked, nodding at Tanner.

"That's Tanner." Cal shook his hand. "You got Mom's order right."

Brody nodded. "Thought so. Her love for peach ice cream was unrivaled by just about anything."

Cal smiled.

"You want something?" Sara asked him.

Brody sighed, staring at the old-fashioned chalk menu.

"A root beer float," India said. "With chocolate ice cream."

Brody chuckled. "Haven't had one of those in a long time."

"Chocolate ice cream?" Cal asked. "Is it good?"

Brody nodded. "Last time I checked, you can't really go wrong with chocolate."

Cal nodded slowly. "Can't argue with that."

India glanced at Brody. He winked, the slight shake of his head so familiar. He'd always had a ready smile and a big, contagious laugh, and a kind word for everyone—and she'd admired him for it. He'd been a refreshing change from the other guys in her life. She and her father had tended to butt heads over every little thing. And the other boys in school were either too full of themselves or too eager to get into her pants to take the time to get to know her.

Of course, things were different now. But she hoped Brody, the man, hadn't outgrown the generous spirit and easy nature she'd held so dear through school.

His gaze was just as thoughtful, just as warm. Which was nice.

Most of the men in her life stirred up other reactions. More like doubt. Insignificance. Defeat. Not that her father meant to undermine and belittle her. But he was a concrete sort of man. It didn't matter if you tried, only if you succeeded.

Unlike JT. If JT was upset or disappointed, his words didn't hurt half as much as his fists. JT had instilled all sorts of cold, hard feelings—fear being right at the top. She hadn't missed him much the last three years.

"Here ya go," Sara said, interrupting her thoughts.

Her hand was shaking as she took her ice-cream cone, so bad she almost dropped it.

"Careful, Mom," Cal said, already scooping into his brownie sundae.

That was the plan. Being careful. As long as she stuck to the plan—save every penny and pass her school counselor certification exam—she and Cal would be on their way to bigger and better things. None of which included staying in Fort Kyle much longer. Until then, she'd be extra careful with her ice cream, her son and her still-battered heart.

BRODY SHOULD HAVE outgrown staring at India Boone like some lovesick teenager. He was a man now. A man with more than his fair share of responsibilities. Responsibilities that included a curmudgeon of a father, a high-strung high-needs mother, almost three-year-old triplets and one hell of a decision to make. He didn't have time to sit beside India Boone, sipping on a root beer float. And watching her savor every lick of her ice cream…well, that was downright dangerous. India Boone had always made his brain short-circuit.

Dammit. He was older, wiser and a little harder now. She should know that, respect that. But one of her impish grins had him downright tongue-tied.

"You know anything about dinosaurs?" Cal asked between bites.

He shook his head, studying the boy. Good-looking kid. No surprise considering who the boy's mother was. "I'm a lawman and a cattleman. Fair to middling on my horse knowledge. But my dinosaur knowledge is rusty." He nodded at the toy sticking out of the boy's pants pocket. "That looks like one poking out of your pocket."

"Plesiosaurus," India said. "That's what that one is called. Cal is a dinosaur expert."

"My daughters are more interested in mermaids than dinosaurs." Brody nodded. "And fairies."

India's brows shot up, her not-so-subtle glance at his left hand making him smile. She hadn't kept up with him, then.

"What's her name?" Cal asked. "Your daughter, I mean?"

"I have three." He smiled. "Suellen, Marilyn and Amberleigh."

"Three?" India asked. "Wow."

He chuckled. "That's about right."

"Where are they?" Cal asked.

"They're at the ranch, with my parents. They love Nana and Granddad," he said.

"Where's their mom?" Cal's question was innocent enough.

"She lives in Houston." Working seventy-hour weeks as the youngest partner at the Law Offices of Hirsch and Martinez. That was who Barbara was. "She'll be out next month for the girls' birthday party. But they Skype most nights, so they can see each other." Barbara worked hard, but she made sure to set aside time just for their girls. And when she visited, she left her work behind.

"Divorced?" Cal asked, waiting for his nod before asking, "Miss her?"

He shrugged. "We're good friends." Which was true. He and Barbara might want different things, but they both wanted the best for the girls.

"I don't see my dad at all anymore," Cal said. "I don't mind."

Brody tried not to look at India. He tried not to react to Cal's matter-of-fact delivery. It didn't work. His gaze met India's—before she turned all of her attention on the remains of her peach ice cream. The look in her eyes made his stomach drop. He didn't like it.

"How long are you visiting?" India asked him, still focused on her ice-cream cone.

"I'm staying put." The corner of his mouth cocked up, waiting for her reaction. They'd made a pact, years ago, to get out—and stay out—of Fort Kyle. Now, here they were, eating the same ice creams and sitting on the same stools they'd always frequented.

"I thought you were some fancy lawyer?" she asked, putting her cone in Cal's empty sundae cup and wiping off her fingers with a napkin.

"I was," he agreed. "Big cars, fancy house, all the bells and whistles." He smiled, shaking his head. "It's not all it's cracked up to be."

His father's heart attack hadn't been unexpected. His dad ate badly, drank too much and refused to exercise. The family doctor had written down a detailed list of the changes he need to make to increase his health *and* posted it on the refrigerator so there was no confusing things. But had Vic Wallace listened? Hell, no. That man was stubborn as a mule. And twice as crotchety.

Since his mother couldn't handle her husband on her own and Brody didn't want the girls raised by a nanny, moving home made sense. Barbara, thankfully, had agreed.

India glanced at him then, her smile back. "You gave that up? And moved back?"

He nodded, wishing her surprise didn't still make him go soft inside. "You?"

"Mom and I live on Papa and Gramma's ranch," Cal offered. "It gets crowded sometimes."

"I'm working at Antiques and Treasures, doing some substitute teaching—until I can take my school counselor certification test." She ran a hand over Cal's close-cropped hair. "It's all temporary."

Brody was sad to hear that. And more than a little curious to know what had brought her back here in the first place. Not that he'd ask—not yet.

"You any good with computers?" Cal asked. "Mom's trying to fix the computer at Gramma's shop."

"Oh?" Brody knew a thing or two about computers.

"I'll figure it out," India interjected, stubborn as always.

"You always tell me to ask for help," Cal grumbled. "You've been trying and trying—"

"And I'll get it," she interrupted, sounding tense.

Brody knew a thing or two about the Boones. India Boone was stubborn as hell—just like her father. Not that he'd dare say such a thing to her.

His cell phone rang, the old-fashioned telephone ringtone echoing in the Soda Shop. "Excuse me," he said. "Brody Wallace," he answered.

He saw Cal's eyes go wide, saw him tugging on his mother's arm and his frantic whisper into her ear.

"Mr. Wallace, this is Rebecca Grant, your father's nurse. He's refusing to do his therapy again. Insurance won't cover my care if he won't comply with doctor's orders." It was the same song and dance every couple of weeks. And one of the reasons Brody had to stay. His mother would wring her hands, cry and call him anyway. Better to deal with it here, in person, head-on.

"Mrs. Grant, I'll head that way now."

"Well, I can't make him, you know that." She sounded exhausted.

His father had that effect on people. "No, ma'am, I know you can't. I'll do the arguing when I get there. You just stay put, I'm coming."

"Yes, sir," she said before the line went dead. He shook his head and shoved his phone into his pocket. "Better head out."

"Your father?" India asked. "Everything all right?" There was concern in her green-blue eyes.

"He's fine. Just being pigheaded is all." He stood. "It was real nice to meet you, Cal."

Cal frowned at him. "It was?"

Brody nodded. "It was."

Cal leaned forward. "Aren't you and Mom supposed to be enemies? You're a Wallace and she's a Boone. Everyone in Fort Kyle knows the Wallaces and Boones don't like each other."

Brody looked at India. "Is that so?" He'd grown up in the shadow of the feud between India's father and his own. It was nonsense, really. His uncle had lost his part of the Wallace ranch to Woodrow Boone in a heated poker game. Woodrow won, he had the deed to prove it, but his father had been crying foul ever since. A few public yelling matches, several fistfights and their never-ending smear campaign against one another had turned a fair, if ridiculous, game of poker into a legendary feud.

India rolled her eyes. "Stop, Brody."

How he loved hearing his name from her lips. "Your papa and my daddy might not get along. But I'll tell you a secret." He leaned forward, whispering loudly. "Your mom is one of my favorite people. I never cared much what her last name was." He paused, glancing at Sara. "But if you're worried about it, Cal, we can keep this quiet."

Sara nodded. "I won't tell a soul."

Cal nodded, smiling. "Probably best. Papa gets loud when he gets upset. And he gets upset a lot." Brody exchanged a grin with India. Cal continued. "'Sides, you're nice. Mom needs nice friends." He patted his mother's hand.

Brody glanced at India again, struck by that distant look in her eyes. She was still smiling, but it was taking effort. He just didn't know why. "I can do that," he said. "Always liked being Goldilocks's best friend." He touched his hat. "I'll be seeing you around. Bet my girls would love to hear all about the dinosaurs, Cal."

"I don't care much for mermaids," Cal said, looking doubtful.

Brody chuckled. "That's okay. Me neither."

"It was so good to see you," India said. "Really."

He smiled. "Maybe we'll run into each other again? Say, Tuesday. The Soda Shop still have a chicken fried steak dinner special on Tuesday, Sara?"

"We sure do," Sara agreed.

"I might just be here around, say, six o'clock on Tuesday, having one. If you two decide you're hungry about that time." He winked at Cal.

Cal smiled. And so did India.

He walked out of the Soda Shop before he did something stupid. Like hug her again. Or ask her to go on a date with him. Or sit there and stare at her...

He was knocked back a few feet, a solid blow to the shoulder catching him by surprise.

"Watch where the hell you're going—" Woodrow Boone broke off, his eyes narrowing.

"My apologies, Mr. Boone." Brody touched his hat. "Didn't see you there."

The man gave him a slow toe-to-head inspection. "Didn't see me? How's that?" He frowned. "Something wrong with your eyes, boy?"

Brody bit back a grin. "No, sir."

Woodrow Boone grunted and pushed past him into the Soda Shop.

"You have a good day," Brody called out, not bothering to wait for a response from his father's self-proclaimed enemy.

Brody climbed into his bright red truck, threw it into

Reverse and headed down Fort Kyle's main drive from town. Miles of dirt roads, cattle guards, cacti and tumble-weeds led him home to Wallace ranch. By the time he'd reached the main house, he'd pushed all thoughts of Wood-row Boone aside. Taking care of his family came first, even if Brody's father was determined to challenge him.

…………… ………
…………………
……………
………………
………………

Chapter Two

"You realize there haven't been fireworks in two years, Brody?" asked Miss Francis, Fort Kyle's busybody with a heart of gold who had the scoop on everyone. "And we're not a stop on the West Texas Rodeo circuit. And the bike race we started a couple years back, to help the fort—it's all but disappeared."

There was no denying this was a sad development. Fort Kyle received only so much money from the state, a fact he knew from serving on the fort's nonprofit board. And losing the rodeo? Rodeo brought in dollars, heads in beds and outside marketing—all good things for a small town off the beaten path. But what the hell was he supposed to do about it? Of all the things to fall on his plate since returning home, Miss Francis had been chosen by some "concerned townsfolk" to convince him he was the town's best option for the upcoming mayoral election.

It wasn't that he wasn't interested, he was. But taking on a task that big would conflict with his current family responsibilities—and there were lots of those. He needed to remember that. He glanced up from where he squatted at his daughter's side, tucking Amberleigh's arm back into her sundress. Amberleigh wasn't fond of clothes. Or shoes. A fact that kept him and his mother trailing after his little girl.

"We've lost the Monarch Festival. Mayor Draper seems to think it's silly." The older woman's sales pitch was interrupted by sweet Marilyn, offering a mud pie with a smile. "Oh, thank you, Marilyn." Miss Francis, a grandmother many times over, took the small plastic plate covered in mud.

Marilyn's grin grew. She was pleased as punch—and covered with mud. "Welcome."

He could imagine his girls chasing after the clouds of monarchs that visited Fort Kyle on their migratory path. The town had always turned their arrival into something special, closing up shops and keeping as many cars off the road as possible to prevent damage to the hundreds of thousands of monarchs. The festival and cattle drive— the short trek from Alpine to Fort Kyle—rounded things out. "How did we lose a festival?" He ran a hand over his face. "Don't eat the mud, Suellen, sweetie."

"'Kay, Daddy." Disappointment lined Suellen's face. But she put her plastic spoon full of mud and dirt back onto her plate.

"Bet Nana has some cookies," he offered, reaching for his coffee cup on the porch step. He took a sip, swallowing the now-cold liquid. Cold coffee was the norm. So were piles of laundry, playing pretend and braiding hair. He was an only child, and his mother was just as clueless about little-girl hairstyles as he was. Since tangles were the enemy, learning to braid had been an essential life skill.

How was he supposed to take care of his daughters, his parents, the ranch *and* Fort Kyle?

Amberleigh was going in circles, trying to pull her arm from her sundress. Lollipop, the white puffball of a dog his wife had given the girls last Christmas, spun along with Amberleigh.

"What's she got against clothes?" Miss Francis asked.

Brody shook his head and stood. "Don't know. But that's the fourth time I've put her dress back on this afternoon."

Miss Francis chuckled. "You don't say?"

"Water those flowers over there, Suellen. Marilyn, you help." He smiled at his girls, nodding at the identical watering cans.

Marilyn was sparing with her water, barely letting a few drops out for each plant.

Suellen started at one end of the flower bed and walked along, sprinkling the soil with a steady light shower of cool well water. Lollipop followed along, his little pink tongue searching for water. Suellen giggled, pouring the last of her water on the dog.

Amberleigh walked to one large sunflower and dumped the entire contents of her watering can on the dirt—making a mud puddle. She dropped her watering can and stooped to scoop out the fresh mud.

He sighed. "Don't dig up Nana's flower, Amberleigh."

"You're quite the multitasker," Miss Francis teased.

"Not like I have a choice. About my family. But running for mayor? Well, that's a horse of a different color." He shot the older woman a look. "Something tells me you're not going to give up."

"Why would I give up?" Miss Francis asked. "Fort Kyle needs young blood and fresh ideas, Brody. You want these girls to grow up having the same experiences you did, don't you?"

Brody shook his head as Amberleigh tugged her dress off and tossed it onto the ground. "I wouldn't have brought them back otherwise." He picked up Amberleigh's dress and followed her across the small fenced yard his mother insisted on keeping green and flowering even when West Texas was fighting drought. "Amberleigh."

His daughter turned, her huge hazel gaze meeting his. She held her hands up and waited. Even with mud streaked down her arms and across one cheek, she was precious. Each of his girls was unique and special. Amberleigh didn't talk much, but that didn't seem to get in her way. He crouched at her side and slid the dress back on. "You don't like your pretty dress?" he asked. Amberleigh shook her head but kissed his cheek.

He hugged her close, breathing in her baby-shampoo scent. Baby shampoo and dirt. "You go make some mud pies with your sisters. Keep your dress on."

Amberleigh nodded and joined her sisters by the large planter he kept dirt in just for them. They had shovels and funnels, various-sized cups—anything to keep them occupied for a while. He sighed. His three girls, barefoot, with mud-streaked clothes, and playing with dirt.

Yes, the girls looked like little angels, but they played hard. Chicken chasers. Puppy groomers. Pillow fort builders—and destroyers. And master mud pie bakers. Something his father found highly amusing, and his mother tolerated. As long as he sprayed off the porch and cleaned up when they were done. He didn't mind—his girls' happiness made cleanup duty worth it.

"Have you talked to Gabe Chasen over at the Tourism Department?" Miss Francis asked.

Brody nodded. Gabe was worried, like Miss Francis, about their small town. Between the fort, the dude ranches, the observatory and how close they were to the Grand Canyon, they should be seeing more tourism dollars. Things like festivals and special events were necessary. And not happening the last two years.

"You know there's a problem, then," Miss Francis pushed.

"I do." He glanced at the older woman, then the back door of the ranch house. "I don't see why I'm the one who needs to fix it. Why don't you run, Miss Francis?"

"Honey, I'm old. And tired. I don't want to be in charge of everyone else's business, but I don't mind getting in the middle of it now and then." She winked. "You can do this, Brody."

"Can do what?" His father walked onto the back porch. "Marilyn, that mud's not for eating."

Brody pulled his handkerchief from his pocket and headed toward his daughter.

"I'm trying to convince your son to run for mayor, Vic." Miss Francis put her hands on her hips. "You know as well as I do John Draper needs to step aside, for the good of our town."

His father grunted. "You thinking about it, Brody? Being mayor?"

Brody considered his father's questions as he cleaned up Marilyn's face. "Marilyn, baby, please don't eat the mud. It's almost dinnertime and we'll eat real food. Okay?"

Marilyn nodded, wiping off her tongue. "Nasty mud." She wrinkled up her little freckle-covered nose.

"Daddy." Suellen held a long, wriggling earthworm between her fingers. "Look."

"You found a friend?" he asked. "Might want to let him go home, Suellen. He lives here, taking care of the flowers."

"He does?" Suellen asked, studying the worm.

"Yes, ma'am. He helps them grow." He ran his hand over Suellen's cheek. "Be gentle with him."

She cradled the worm in both hands then, stooping

to carefully place the worm back in the soil Amberleigh had saturated. "Good, Daddy?"

"Perfect, baby." He smiled, nodded and turned to face his father. "I've been thinking about it. Miss Francis hasn't given me much choice." He glanced at the grinning older woman. "What do you think, Dad? About me running? I've been gone for a while—"

"You've always been a Fort Kyle boy, Brody. Even if you did hang your hat in Houston for a while. You came home," Miss Francis argued.

"Dad?" Brody pushed. If he did this, and it was a big *if*, he'd want his father's support.

His father stared at him, considering his words. Which meant he was thinking of the right thing to say. "You want to do it, you should."

Brody sighed. His father had lumped him into the defector camp the day he'd left for law school. Vic Wallace had money, and his son didn't need to go off to make more—that was what he'd told Brody anyway. But Brody needed to find his own way, become his own man, and leaving had been the best way for him to do that. He didn't regret going. Or coming back.

"I'm not sure," he confessed, glancing at his girls. "Got plenty to keep me busy right now."

His father snorted. "You think it'll get easier when you have three teenage girls running around? Live your life, boy. Fort Kyle'd be lucky to have you for mayor."

The hint of pride in his father's voice was the best endorsement Brody could ask for.

His father burst out laughing. "Besides, I can't wait to see Woodrow Boone's face when a Wallace is mayor."

And there it was. Brody frowned, his gaze returning to his daughters. He had no expectation when it came to India Boone, he knew better. The bad blood between their fathers was too full of vitriol to allow their long-term secret friendship to become public. Or for India to ever discover how deeply he'd loved her for the past fourteen years.

INDIA SAT AT the table in the back corner of Fort Kyle's small library. Her textbooks, notes and laptop covered the table, along with an array of highlighters, pens and pencils. She'd been reviewing her best practices for school counseling prevention and intervention for the last two hours, and her head was starting to spin.

She had five weeks until her test. Once she passed, she could apply for a full-time counseling position—which she was more likely to find in the city. She'd never be rich, but she and Cal wouldn't have to stay here, being a burden to her father. That was what she wanted: choices. For the last few years, her fate had been determined by someone else. From now on, she would be the one to decide her fate. And when she stood on her own two feet, she wanted it to be away from her dad's judgment and scrutiny. A positive fresh start for her and Cal—in a place where her father's unwavering disappointment wouldn't have her questioning her decisions and weighing her down. She could be a better person—a better mother—if she wasn't living in the shadow of a painful past her father still blamed her for.

"Mom," Cal said from the beanbag in the corner. "I'm hungry." Tanner, whom the librarian kindly turned a blind eye on, sprawled on his patch of carpet, snoring.

She glanced at her watch. "You're always hungry, Cal." But it was 6:13 p.m. Dinnertime.

He chuckled. "I'm a growing boy, Mom."

She glanced at her son, already taller than most boys his age. "Don't I know it?" JT had been tall. And broad.

And strong. All nice traits. Thankfully, that was where the resemblance ended. He'd just turned two when JT left, so Cal had been spared most of his father's mercurial mood swings. But India remembered things all too clearly. How jealous he'd been about Cal, how frustrated he'd been by their infant son's tears and how needy the new baby was. Thinking of how he'd yanked Cal from his high chair on one particular occasion still knocked the breath from her lungs. She'd managed to get her baby into the safety of his room and locked him inside before JT turned violent. The marks he'd left on her that night must have scared him, too, because JT had left the next day. The divorce papers she'd received six months later was the last she'd heard of him. She hoped it stayed that way.

"Are we going to the Soda Shop?" Cal asked.

She started packing up her things. "For dinner?"

"It's Tuesday," he said. "Isn't it?"

She nodded, powering off her laptop.

"Chicken fried steak. With your...*friend*?" He glanced over his shoulder, making sure no one was listening.

"Cal." She giggled, instantly remembering Brody's offer. "He was kidding." Surely he had been? Besides, she wasn't sure it was a good idea. Not because of their fathers or their ridiculous feud, but because she needed to stay strong—without leaning on Brody's broad shoulders. "Do you want chicken fried steak?" she asked, zipping up her backpack.

He shrugged. "I don't want brisket." Which was standard Tuesday fare at her parents' dude ranch.

"I'll take that as a yes." She glanced at her watch again. It was after six. Chances were, he'd eaten and left. If he'd even shown up. "Okay. Let's go."

"Come on, boy," Cal said, patting his side. Tanner hopped up, instantly ready to go.

They strolled down the stone sidewalk. The walk from the library to the Soda Shop was short—nothing was far in town. They said hello to their neighbors, watched the storefronts closing up and crossed the street to get to the Soda Shop. She ignored the sudden onset of nerves that gripped her as she pushed through the door. It was just Brody, after all.

"Maybe he didn't come," Cal said, glancing around the restaurant.

"We can still have dinner." She nudged him, smiling. "Even if it's just me."

He smiled up at her. "I don't mind."

"Miss Boone," Sara greeted them from the bar. "You two here for dinner? Pick a table and I'll bring you some menus. I might even have a bone or two for Tanner."

Cal waved at the teenager. "Thanks, Sara. Let's get a booth, Mom." He led her to a booth on the far side of the restaurant. Tanner sat at the end of the table, staring at them. "Sara's checking on something special, boy."

They were just seated when a little girl came walking down the hall. Her long strawberry blond pigtails bounced above her shoulders. She had pink embroidered jean shorts on. But she was wearing no shoes.

"Amberleigh," a voice called after her. "Shoes."

The little girl stopped, sighed and walked back down the hallway.

"You think she's lost?" Cal asked.

India grinned. She had a pretty good idea whom the little girl belonged to. Besides the little girl's red-gold curls, India recognized the man's voice. That precious barefoot toddler had to belong to Brody Wallace. Which meant he *was* here.

A few seconds later, Brody appeared—followed by three absolutely adorable little girls.

He stopped when he saw her, smiling widely at her quick back-and-forth inspection of his daughters. "Yep, they're mine," he said.

"I can see that," she returned, marveling how similar they were. Similar, but not identical. "Wow. I mean, really, wow."

He nodded. "Yep. India, Cal, these are my girls. This is Marilyn."

Marilyn wore a headband and had a light dusting of freckles and a quick smile.

"And Suellen," he said, patting his other daughter's shoulder.

Suellen's hair curled up tight, two tiny bows—one on each side of her head—and a dimple in her left cheek.

"And Amberleigh," he finished.

Amberleigh had lopsided pigtails, lots of freckles and a slow, shy smile. She'd been the shoeless one.

"It's nice to meet you," India said. Brody had kids. Three girls. Would they ever know how lucky they were to have him for a father?

"Your dog?" Marilyn asked, pointing at Tanner.

"He's big," Suellen said, hiding behind Brody's leg.

"This is Tanner," Cal said. "He's a real good dog."

But the two little girls didn't look convinced. Only Amberleigh approached Tanner, smiling as the dog sniffed her all over before licking her cheek. Amberleigh giggled.

"I didn't think you'd come," Brody said, one brow arching and the corner of his mouth kicking up. Almost embarrassed.

"You asked us," Cal said, matter-of-fact.

"Daddy," Marilyn spoke up. "Color?"

"You sure can, darlin'." Brody pulled back a chair at a table next to their booth. "Climb on up and we'll get you girls situated. Thing is, my folks decided to invite themselves. I imagine they'll be along shortly."

Meaning she and Cal would not be enjoying the pleasure of Brody's adorable girls for dinner. Not unless Vic Wallace had decided to stop blaming her father for stealing his family's land. As ridiculous as the feud was, she didn't deny that the insult to her father—and her family name—stung.

"That's nice," India said, watching as Brody pulled coloring books and crayons from his beaten leather messenger bag.

Brody made a face. "I guess."

She giggled.

"Fairies? Mermaids?" Cal frowned at the girls' coloring books. "And dragons." His disapproval lessened. "Who likes dragons?"

"Amberleigh," Suellen said. "Dragons. And mud."

"No clothes. Or shoes," Marilyn added.

India shot Brody a grin. He shrugged.

"Dragons are cool." Not that Cal was fully on board.

"Color?" Suellen asked. "There's a scary fairy picture I don' wanna color."

"Scary?" Cal asked, peering at the picture Suellen showed him. "She is mean looking."

Amberleigh proceeded to make the mean fairy face. Suellen and Marilyn covered their faces with their napkins, but Cal only grinned at the scowling little girl. Which made Amberleigh giggle again.

"That's twice," Brody said, smiling at his daughter. "Just about the sweetest sound imaginable."

The tenderness on his face was too much for her. So she focused on his little girls, diligently coloring, instead. "They're gorgeous."

Amberleigh waved Cal forward and patted the chair

beside her, holding her coloring book. "Mom?" Cal asked India.

"Amberleigh doesn't share her coloring book with just anyone," Brody said.

"Just until we order." Which probably wasn't the smartest answer—considering his folks were on the way. But, resisting Amberleigh's offer was plain wrong. Cal climbed into the chair beside Amberleigh, and conversation came to a stop. All four kids were coloring quietly, happily preoccupied.

Leaving her and Brody, sitting next to her at his table. Her nerves returned. Now they'd have that awkward what-have-you-been-doing-with-your-life conversation she dreaded. She'd gone to school, gotten married, had Cal and divorced. Now she was back home. Not exactly riveting conversation.

Considering they were both back in the place they'd been so determined to leave, it was clear things hadn't gone according to plan for either of them.

But she had questions for her one-time best friend. Like, what did she do to make you divorce her? India knew without asking that Brody hadn't done a thing. He was a good guy, always had been—always would be. Even though he was much taller and larger and all man, he had the same kind eyes and warm smile. He was handsome in a way any woman would appreciate. Whoever his ex-wife was, she was an idiot.

"What's a fancy-pants lawyer like you going to do with all your free time?" she asked, diving in. Had he chosen to leave his high-power, big-money job in Houston, or had something happened that made him leave?

"Well, you're looking at a good portion of it." He leaned back, long legs sprawled out in front of him. He sort of spilled out of the wooden chair, too big and broad for it. "The ranch won't run itself, either. And the grocery and feed stores will need looking in on now and then." He shrugged, glancing her way, then away.

When they'd been younger, that look meant he was holding out on her. "Why do I get the feeling there's more?"

He shrugged again, smiling this time.

"As I live and breathe, a Boone and a Wallace sitting down and working together?" Miss Francis's startled question caught her and Brody by surprise. "I'm all for ending the feud, but you might want to build up to it first. I just saw your folks parking out front, Brody."

India's stomach churned with anxiety and frustration. She'd grown up knowing the Wallaces were stubborn, mean-spirited people. But she'd never thought about Brody as one of *them*. He was just Brody.

"Cal," she said, calling her son back to their booth—across from Brody and his girls. "We should order. I don't want you up too late."

Cal handed Amberleigh the crayon. "I'll finish next time." He stepped over Tanner and slid into the booth.

Amberleigh frowned but took the crayon. She slumped in her chair, crossed her arms over her chest and huffed out a big sigh.

India tried her hardest not to laugh.

"India, you don't have to—"

"She's still wearing her clothes, Ramona. No need to worry," Vic Wallace announced as he entered the Soda Shop. "Your mother was fretting the whole ride. Francis, why are you everywhere I look?"

"You're just lucky, I guess," Francis answered.

The man had aged. She had few memories of Vic Wallace. When she'd been little, she'd been scared of him. He'd been taller than her father, his fiery red hair making him appear all the more hot-tempered. Her father wasn't a small man, but something about Mr. Wallace had seemed…looming. And when he got riled up, his red face would rival his red hair. Her father tended to make sure Vic Wallace's face was blazing red before he walked away.

When Ramona Wallace glanced at their table, India did her best to appear absorbed in her menu. Like Cal. He read well enough for a five-year-old—he wouldn't need help choosing his dinner. "Not getting the chicken fried steak?" she asked.

"Just seeing what else they have." He grinned at her. "But I think I'll go with the steak."

"Sounds good," India said.

"Done coloring?" Miss Francis was talking to Amberleigh.

Amberleigh had stopped coloring and was now peeling all the labels from her crayons. A shoe sat on the table, by the little girl's fork.

"Amberleigh, put your shoe back on, sweetheart." Mrs. Wallace was embarrassed more than anything.

The little girl picked up her shoe, tried to put it back on, then tossed it in frustration. The white slip-on went flying, landing on the floor in front of Tanner. Tanner sat up, glanced at the shoe, then Cal. It took every ounce of India's control not to laugh. Brody was fighting the same battle. She saw it in those clear toffee eyes of his.

But the expressions on Ramona's and Vic Wallace's faces, on Miss Francis's, were simply hilarious. She giggled, pressing her napkin to her mouth to stifle it.

Brody, she noticed, was clearing his throat behind her.

Cal studied the shoe, then Amberleigh. He slipped from the booth and picked up her shoe. "Lose your shoe?" he asked.

"She threw it, Cal," Marilyn offered. "Don't like them."

"Hit your dog?" Suellen asked, hiding behind her napkin again.

"Nope. Tanner is fine," he said, slipping from his seat and walking to Amberleigh. "Want it?"

Amberleigh shook her head, but there were tears in the little girl's eyes. And India couldn't stop herself from joining her son. "Want Cal to help you put it on?"

Amberleigh stared at her with wide hazel eyes. India could only imagine what was going on in that little head of hers. "Don't like 'em," Amberleigh announced.

"Your shoes?" India asked, taking the shoe from Cal and peering inside. "I had shoes like this when I was little. They pinched and made my toes feel squished."

Amberleigh watched her closely.

"Is that the problem?" Brody asked. "We can get you new shoes, darlin'."

Amberleigh shook her head. "Don't like 'em."

"Don't blame you," Cal said, sounding off. "Barefoot's always better. Unless you're working outside." He placed the shoe back on the table.

Amberleigh smiled at Cal again, offering him more of her newly peeled crayons.

"Not in a restaurant, it's not," Vic Wallace said, recovering from his embarrassment to scowl in Cal's direction.

She stiffened. He could be as rude as he wanted to be to her father—or her. But her son was another matter. She urged Cal back to their table and sat, smiling his way.

"The boy's trying to help," Miss Francis said.

"No help needed. *She* needs to learn to keep her shoes on," Mr. Wallace grumbled. "It's ridiculous."

India watched Amberleigh slump farther down in her seat.

"Vic," Mrs. Wallace scolded, softly.

"I'm so hungry I could eat a cow," Brody said, making the girls laugh. "Or a hippopotamus."

"Or a ephelant?" Marilyn asked.

"Elephant?" Brody nodded.

"Or…or a whale?" Suellen asked.

"Maybe," Brody agreed, winking at them. "I'll ask Sara if there's whale on the menu."

The three girls "aahed" in unison, their little noses wrinkling up in distaste.

"We should celebrate. Sara, get the little ones here a milk shake," Mr. Wallace said. "Not every day your son decides to run for mayor. We'll run a big campaign, plaster the name *Wallace* all over the place."

Brody for mayor?

"Might run." Brody glanced her way.

He'd do a good job—because he was a good man.

"Time to make a decision. There's not a single reason to stop you, Brody," his father said.

Brody glanced her way again. "I can think of a few. Besides, I'm not much of politician, Dad. What you see is what you get."

"That's why at least half of Fort Kyle wants you, Brody. There's no one else in these parts with the experience you have." Miss Francis seemed to be his biggest fan. "You'd do good things. Be fair."

India agreed, but she didn't say a word. Brody would make this town proud and make the town a place to be proud of.

"And you'd make your daddy happy." Miss Francis nudged Vic Wallace in the side, earning a small smile from the man.

India had given up trying to make her father happy—it was impossible. Besides, something this big shouldn't be about one person. It was a lot to take in, to consider. Especially for a single father of three.

She was a single mother to the smartest, kindest, most patient five-year-old in the universe, and it was tough.

Brody's sigh drew India's attention his way. There was a slight furrow on his brow, like he was working through something complicated. Did he want this? If there was one thing the last few years had taught her, it was to follow your instinct.

Clearly, Brody was conflicted. Did he have someone to talk to, to weigh the pros and cons of such a monumental job? Did he have someone special? Or was he lonely, like her?

Her phone alarm jingled, reminding her to pick up milk on the way home and jarring her from thoughts of Brody and his life choices. Brody Wallace was part of her past, not her future. If he was serious about running for mayor, her father would consider that an act of war. Being Brody's friend—an act of treason.

Chapter Three

Brody rode around the near-dry water tank. The ground wasn't baked dry enough to crack yet, but it was coming. Texas weather was erratic, arctic cold to blazing heat—in the span of a day. But occasionally they had a nice in-between. Like today. A cooling breeze, bright blue sky and fluffy clouds towering up and casting long, slow-moving shadows on the ground beneath his feet.

"We could use a good rain." He spoke to his horse, Bear.

The massive buckskin snorted in reply.

He chuckled, tipping his hat forward to shield his gaze from the glare of the sun. He scanned the horizon carefully.

A pack of wild pigs had come through the back property, tearing through the fences and digging ruts to keep cool. Besides being mean-tempered, the animals could cause a hell of a lot of damage to property. The game warden had called and asked him to keep an eye out, but Brody had yet to see them.

A distant whip-poor-will sang out, making Bear's ears perk up and Brody search the blooming cactus, mesquite and grasses for some sign of the bird. No luck; the bird was camouflaged well.

Out here, things were clear-cut and simple. He could

whittle through what he wanted and what he needed and envision what his future could be. A future that included things like happy daughters, healthy parents and a loving woman at his side.

He knew who he wanted that woman to be. But, even out here, he had no idea how to make that work.

She was beautiful. But the world knew that. Head cheerleader, prom queen and Miss Fort Kyle Cattle Queen four years in a row. The girls liked her. And the boys lined up to date her. He'd grown up seeing her for who she was—an awkward lonely girl who'd just wanted to be one of the crowd. Not looked up to or fawned over, but accepted.

His mission was to be that person for her. It hadn't happened overnight. Hell, it probably wouldn't have happened at all if her father hadn't made him off-limits. Nothing spurs a teenage girl into action like her father's disapproval. Surprisingly, their friendship had become important to both of them. But what had started out as friendship turned into something more for him, something he'd never been able to shake, something India never knew about.

When she'd headed to Texas Women's University in Dallas, he'd headed for University of Texas in Austin. The distance had changed things.

College, law school, Barbara, his career and the girls. Life had kept him too busy to think much beyond what was right in front of him. When he'd decided to bring the girls here, he'd made the choice to make time for the things that mattered. Like his girls. His parents.

And now, maybe, India.

He and Bear headed back to the ranch and straight for the barn. He stored his saddle and bridle, brushed Bear's coat and made sure to clean out his hooves before turning the horse into the large pasture behind the barn.

"How's it look?" His father joined him at the fence. "They're saying we might get a shower or two end of the week. That'd help."

Brody nodded, inspecting the sky. "Depends. We need a good soaking, not a flash flood."

"I'll take what I get, son." He clapped him on the shoulder. "Water's water."

Which was true, but a hard, fast rain eroded just as much as drought. "The well looks good. If the tank dries out, we'll fill the troughs. We'll be fine. Like always."

His father nodded. "Chance of heading into town? Your mother got a package needs to be picked up. Maybe stop in, check on Willie, see how he's running the store." His father leaned against the fence, doing his best to act casual.

"Can do," he agreed. On top of the ranch, the Wallaces owned the local grocery store and feed store. Both were successful, thriving businesses his father oversaw personally. But now, with his health, it was too much. His father had a hard time asking for help—that was one of the reasons he'd come home. If his father wanted something done, and he often had a roundabout way of asking, Brody would do it.

"Give Mom a hand with the girls?"

The older man nodded. "Can do. Maybe check in at the bakery, see if they've got some of that peach cobbler for dessert. Don't tell your mother, though."

Brody chuckled. "Can do." His mother wasn't much of a baker, but neither of them would ever say as much.

He walked his father back to the house, kissed the girls on the head and headed into town with a grocery list from his mother—and Amberleigh. By the time they'd reached Wallace Family Grocery, Amberleigh had tugged off her boots and her socks. But she was happy, her little feet bouncing along with the George Strait songs coming through his radio.

"Shopping for Nana?" Amberleigh asked when they'd parked in front of the grocery store.

"Yes, ma'am," he said, carrying her inside. "Wanna ride?"

She nodded, sliding her legs through the grocery cart opening. "Go fast, Daddy."

He grinned, pushing the cart down the aisle at a slow jog. Amberleigh squealed with glee, her little eyes shut and her head tilted back. Until they rounded a corner and came to a screeching halt a few feet from an old woman pushing her cart.

The old woman scowled and kept on going, moving at a snail's pace.

"That was some look," he said to Amberleigh. "Think we're in trouble?"

Amberleigh nodded. "Scary fairy."

Brody burst out laughing at the comparison of the old lady and the mean fairy in their coloring books. "Pretty close, Amberleigh. Pretty close."

He stopped in the office, talked to Willie and let Amberleigh ride on the coin-operated horse by the ice-cream section.

"Like Bear, Daddy." His daughter smiled. "Giddy-up, horsey."

"Don't let him get away from you." He winked at her.

Her hold tightened on her reins. "Whoa."

"Good job." He nodded. His father had purchased ponies for the girls, but only Amberleigh had been interested. Marilyn had refused. Suellen was more interested in petting it and sneaking the pony carrots and apples.

He knew they were fraternal triplets, but he'd never expected the girls to be so different.

Not that he'd have it any other way.

"All done." She reached for him, laughing when he swung her around and deposited her back into the cart.

"Time to get some shopping done." He set off again.

He turned shopping into a game, sneaking around corners and dodging all the other carts. All it took was his daughter's laugh to keep him going. He figured her sisters talked so much Amberleigh didn't feel the need to join in. Hearing her talk was a rare treat.

They loaded the groceries into the truck. But the sight of India disappearing inside Antiques and Treasures made him pause.

INDIA HIT ENTER on the computer keyboard. Nothing. The prompt popped up again, so she reentered the access code—rechecking each keystroke before moving on. If it took the entire hour she had before Cal got out of school, so be it. She could do this. She would do it. She hit Enter again.

"Come on," she said, frowning at the computer screen. "Please."

"Pretty sure manners won't make much of a difference," Brody said from the doorway, startling her so that she knocked her bottle of water from the desk and into her lap. "Damn, India, I'm so sorry." He was across the room in an instant, offering his handkerchief.

"It was an accident," she said, pushing out of her chair. "There wasn't much left anyway. It was…refreshing. And cold."

He shook his head, eyeing her pants.

"It's okay," she assured him, resting her hand on his

arm. "It's water. Not a national security crisis. Or a stupid software problem."

His hand covered hers. "I might be able to help with the computer. Make up for dousing you with cold water?"

His hand was warm. His arm was warm. Even the look in his tawny gaze was warm. And it washed over her, from the tips of her toes to the top of her head. A peculiar tightening settled deep in her stomach.

"Will it get me out of the doghouse?" he asked.

She swallowed. "If you're offering to help me not throw this piece of junk into the trash, I'm not going to complain about getting a little water on my pants." She glanced down at her pants. "Okay, more than a little water."

Brody chuckled, his eyes crinkling at the corners.

India wasn't sure what was happening, but it was good. All the warmth and the touching and the smiling… She should let go of him.

"Let me see what I can do," he offered, moving toward the computer—and taking his warmth with him.

This was weird. Brody was, had been, her friend. She'd never stared at his broad shoulders before. Or, when he climbed under her desk, his rear. But now, India was completely distracted by pretty much everything about Brody. It was unnerving as hell. But not necessarily bad.

"Looks like the modem was plugged in incorrectly," he said, sitting back on his knees and inspecting the back of the modem.

"Of course it was." She shook her head. "Please don't tell me I've spent the last week stressing out over nothing."

He grinned up at her. "If it was stressing you out, it was something." He'd always been good at that—making things better. "Let's try it now." He tucked the modem back into place, then sat in her chair. "Aw, shit."

She covered her mouth, laughing at the wet spot soaking the back of his pants. And his mighty-fine rear. "Um, it might still be a little wet."

He cocked a brow. "Thanks." With a shake of his head, he sat and focused on the task at hand. His expression changed, eyes narrowing, lips quirked, his jaw going rigid as he plugged in the codes. With a few more clicks, the screen turned blue and the welcome popped up. "Looks like it took."

"That was it? A plug? Really?" She glanced back and forth between him and the computer screen. "I don't know whether to hug you or hit you."

He stood. "I'd prefer a hug. A hug is the better choice."

She laughed, hugging him before she had time to think it through. "Thank you, Brody. You have no idea how frustrated I've been."

His arms were strong and secure around her. "Life's too short to sweat the small stuff."

She nodded, far too content to stay in his arms. "You were right," she whispered, trying not to burrow closer. It was hard.

"About not sweating the small stuff?" he asked. "Can't take the credit. It's one of those inspirational quote-of-the-day things."

"Not that." She laughed again. "About the hug."

"Oh." His arms tightened. "That. Yeah, I'm enjoying it. You always gave good hugs."

She gave up the fight and burrowed closer. "I was going to say the same thing." The problem was she didn't want to let go.

"You okay, Goldilocks?" he asked, his voice close to her ear.

"Of course." Was she? She was trying to be. Maybe her hold on him was a little too tight, a little too needy, to be convincing.

"I think we should load up the truck and head out to the ridge—like we used to," he said. "A little stargazing and solving the world's problems." His breath brushed her ear.

"Think it'll work?" she asked.

"Might be worth a try." His hand stroked her back.

Except they were no longer teenagers. They were adults. Parents. With very different goals. Hers was to get out of Fort Kyle. His was to become mayor.

"Um, hi." India's sister, Scarlett, stood awkwardly in the doorway, Amberleigh in her arms. "She was looking for her daddy."

India stiffened. At least it was Scarlett. She wouldn't say a word to anyone—not that there was anything to tell.

"You need to get a doorbell or something," Brody said, letting go of India. "Or someone could sneak up on you and scare you."

India laughed in spite of herself.

"We didn't mean to scare you, did we?" Scarlett asked Amberleigh.

Amberleigh shook her head. "Brought cookies, Daddy."

"Thank you, darlin'." Brody crossed the room to his daughter.

India watched as he stooped, taking the cookie his little girl held up. Maybe his hug had reinforced just how lonely she was. Maybe it was because Brody was synonymous with comfort and security. Or maybe it was because he was incredibly attractive. It was probably a combination. Whatever the reason, she couldn't shake this new awareness of Brody.

"Share, Daddy," the little girl said. "Manners."

Brody broke the cookie evenly, offering India half.

The brush of his fingers against hers was far too potent for her liking. "That's right, Amberleigh. Manners are important," India agreed.

Amberleigh smiled. "Where's Cal?"

"He's still at school." She grinned.

Amberleigh nodded.

"In a few years, you'll be at school, too," Scarlett said. "You'll see Cal all the time. And bunches of other kids."

Amberleigh perked up.

She'd have to talk to Brody about the half-day pre-K program the school offered. Amberleigh was smart and busy and ready for more social interaction. "Lose your shoes again?" India asked, smiling at the little girl.

Amberleigh shook her head. "Daddy's truck."

"I pick my battles," Brody said, winking at her.

India tried not to stare.

But Brody's gaze held hers, and his jaw tightened.

"Want me to go put Amberleigh in the truck?" Scarlett asked. "Or wait outside?"

Heat singed her chest, up her neck and cheeks. "He fixed my computer."

"After I spilled water all over her," he interjected.

"The hug was a…thank-you?" Scarlett didn't buy it. But she smiled. "That's all?"

"What else would it be?" Brody asked. "I've got too much sense to fall for a woman who has no intention of staying put." He scooped up Amberleigh. "We'd better head out soon or your grandparents will run for the hills."

"Thank you, Brody," India said, waving them off.

Scarlett waited until they'd gone before turning a wide-eyed gaze her way. "You know, Fort Kyle is a good place, India. I'd love it if you stayed. So would Mom. I know you and Dad don't always see eye-to-eye, but that won't change whether you stay here or go. Don't let him steal your chance at a very good thing." She pointed out the large window at Brody and Amberleigh. "That right there is a very good thing."

India watched Brody pack his little girl into his truck, her sister's words more tempting than they should've been.

Chapter Four

"What in tarnation is happening to this town?" her father asked, slamming the newspaper down on the breakfast table hard enough to make the glasses shudder and the cutlery clink.

"What's the matter, dear?" her mother asked, unruffled by his outburst.

"That boy, that Wallace boy, is running for mayor? There's an official press release," he thundered. "What is he thinking? Why, he hasn't even been in Fort Kyle long enough to run, has he?"

He'd done it. Brody Wallace was officially running for mayor of Fort Kyle. And, after spending the last few months listening to her father hem and haw over the current mayor, he stood a very good chance of winning. Even with the last name *Wallace*. India caught Cal's eye. He winked at her, chewing his pancakes with enthusiasm.

"He's a lawyer, isn't he?" Scarlett asked. "He's really nice, Dad—"

"Really nice?" her father interrupted. "A snake in the grass, I'll bet. Just like his father. Full of venom, too."

Scarlett glanced at her and tried again. "Click knows him pretty well—"

"Click Hale?" he snapped. "Hmph. I know he up and married your cousin Tandy, but that doesn't magically erase his past. Makes sense he and the Wallace boy would be friends."

"*Click's* past?" India asked, her patience vanishing. Why she let her father get to her was a mystery she'd yet to solve. She wasn't normally adversarial. But she and her father couldn't seem to avoid ending every conversation with an argument. In this case it was justified. Her father was too quick to label and criticize. Now he wanted to judge the sons on the sins of their fathers. Click. *And* Brody. "Click Hale never did anything to anyone—except marry Tandy. And I'm pretty sure that was one hundred percent voluntary on both their parts. His parents' drama shouldn't be his burden to bear."

All eyes were on her.

"You turn everything I say into an argument."

She stared at him. *She* did?

"When did you get so fond of Click Hale?" her father asked.

"The day he became family," she countered. "You're the one who says blood is thicker than water."

"Let's try to have a peaceable breakfast," her mother pleaded. "Cal, would you pass the toast, please?"

Cal nodded, passing the towering plate of toast to the other end of the table.

"Besides, Woodrow, I wouldn't worry too much about Brody Wallace, dear. Mayor Draper's done a fine job." Her mother took a piece of toast. "I'm sure he's not going anywhere."

"No, in point of fact, Draper has not." Her father stared at the newspaper. "The last few years he's gotten downright lazy, and Fort Kyle's suffered for it."

India glanced at her father then, hearing the slight strain to his normally booming voice. He'd never hinted that their financial security was in jeopardy.

"Maybe a change is good?" Scarlett asked.

Her father scowled. "Maybe. If the change wasn't named Wallace."

India sighed, loudly, and rolled her eyes. "Why don't you run, then?"

Her mother made an odd choking noise that had Scarlett patting her on the back.

Her father shook his head. "I've no interest in politics. I'm a little too rough around the edges, as you have all pointed out on more than one occasion."

They all smiled then.

"Should we give him a chance, Papa? Mom says it's important to give everyone a chance." Cal shoved a huge bite of pancake into his mouth then.

Her father grunted. "Look how well that turned out when she married—"

"I think that's a lovely idea," Scarlett interrupted.

India chose to ignore her father's reminder that she'd married a man he'd never approved of and moved on. "Does he have a solid platform?"

"He's got little kids," Scarlett said. "He'll be thinking about their future."

Her father grunted again. "Where's his wife? A man who can't commit can't be trusted."

"Well, dear?" her mother asked. "What is Mr. Wallace's campaign platform?"

Her father glared at all of them before opening his paper. "Bringing tourism dollars back to the area, cleaning up and updating the schools and renovating the seniors' community center with increased programming." He snorted.

India exchanged a look with her sister and mother.

"Sounds smart," her mother said. "Something for the

young, something for the old and something the whole town needs."

"He always was smart," Scarlett said. "And nice."

"He is," Cal agreed.

"When did you meet Brody Wallace?" her father asked.

"In the Soda Shop," Cal answered, his cheeks and ears turning bright red. "He said hi to Mom and me."

Her father glanced her way. "Don't go getting friendly with the Wallaces just to spite me."

India put her napkin on her plate and stood. "Dad, believe it or not, I don't take joy in getting your blood pressure elevated. I didn't think exchanging hellos with the man would be a problem. We went to school together, we're not strangers." She left it at that. For now. "Cal, you ready for school?"

Cal shoved the last of his pancakes into his mouth and nodded, pushing his chair back.

"Are you working at the school today?" her mother asked.

"No. My test is coming up so I thought I'd head to the library to study. Unless you need me at the shop?" she asked.

"Not this morning." She paused. "Could you come in after you pick up Cal? Just for a few hours? I need to get my hair touched up."

With a nod at her mother, a quick hug for her sister and a stilted wave for her father, she and Cal headed out.

"Tanner?" Cal called, smiling as the large dog came barreling around the front porch and jumped into the backseat of the truck.

"Ready to go to town?" she asked, rubbing the dog behind both ears before climbing into the truck.

"Papa was sure in a mood this morning," Cal said, slamming the truck door behind him.

"The name *Wallace* has always had that effect on him." She started the truck, pulled onto the main road and headed into town.

They chatted the rest of the drive. Cal had to make a diorama for school, and he was determined to work a dinosaur into it—one way or another she knew he'd have the most impressive project in class. She pressed a kiss to his cheek as they pulled up in front of the school.

"Be good." Not that Cal needed reminding. He was, always, good as gold.

He nodded. "You, too, Mom," he called back to her. "Study hard."

She watched him hurry inside, pulling forward only when the doors closed behind him. Tanner whimpered, so India patted him on the side. "He'll be home soon."

She navigated the quiet streets of Fort Kyle, bought a large coffee at the tiny diner that was open early and headed to the library. The streets were quiet, the sky shot through with a dozen shades of pink and blue, and the air was crisp and cool. She loved mornings like this—in Fort Kyle. The library wasn't open yet, but Helen Jones, the librarian, would let her in so she had a nice, quiet place to study.

The amount of cars and trucks parked in front of the library was a surprise, but she didn't let it slow her down. She pushed inside, Tanner at her side, and paused at the table set up right inside the doors. Among the group gathered, she recognized Miss Francis—and the woman waved her over.

"Well, I'll be," Miss Francis said. "Don't tell me you're here to volunteer for Brody's race for mayor?"

India shook her head. "N-no. I came to study."

"Good for you, India. A gal needs to be able to take care of herself these days."

India nodded. "That's the plan. And Cal, too."

She hadn't realized Brody had joined them until he said, "I admire an independent woman." He was so tall she had to tilt her head back to see him.

"Morning," she said.

"Morning. Coffee?" He stooped, inhaling. "Smells good."

She held the coffee closer. "It is. And necessary for me to be remotely productive today."

He chuckled. "Understood. Hands off the coffee."

"So, is this headquarters now?" she asked.

He shook his head. "No, this is just a meet and greet."

"His first public appearance." Miss Francis tilted her head. "You're missing something. A tie?"

He frowned, running a hand over the pressed front of his blue button-up. It made his tawny eyes pop. "A tie?"

India laughed. "You make it sound like a dirty word."

He chuckled again, eyes sparkling. "It is. They're damn uncomfortable."

"Then don't wear one," she said, shaking her head. Had he always been this handsome? Surely not. She would have remembered it. Yes, all of her memories of Brody Wallace were pleasant, but not heart thumping. Not like this.

She wasn't aware of the fact that they were staring at each other, not really, not until Miss Francis cleared her throat.

"Well, I should let you get back to doing whatever you're doing," she said, taking two steps back and colliding with a person behind her. "Sorry," she said, glancing over her shoulder, and then stepping forward again.

Brody's hands gripped her shoulders. "We'll try to

keep it quiet, so you can study. Chances are, no one will turn up." He squeezed once, and let her go.

Miss Francis laughed then. "You take a gander out that window, boy. I'd say we're heading for standing room only."

India glanced out the front window to see the parking lot filling up. "Good luck," she whispered.

"Wouldn't need luck if I had coffee," he said, smiling widely.

With a sigh, she handed him her coffee. "You owe me."

He took the cup, his smile slow and sweet. "I do. And I look forward to repaying you."

BRODY TOOK THE tie off and handed it back to the volunteer who had lent it to him an hour ago. He'd smiled for the cameras, answered dozens of questions and, he hoped, sounded like a respectable candidate for mayor. When his return to help his father came up, talk of his daughters and his divorce were briefly touched on. He was single and had three daughters—both were public knowledge. Dating status and what he might be looking for in a new wife were questions he laughed off.

He had no interest in dating right now.

With one exception.

"You did well," Miss Francis said. "Real well. It helps that you're so damn cute."

He shook his head. "What's next?"

"The Monarch Festival committee is meeting in three days. Might be a good idea for you to show up, do what you can to make sure it's back on track, and ingratiate yourself with those on the committee. Mostly women, of course, but it can't hurt. Many a man listens to his wife when behind closed doors." She grinned. "You up for it?"

He nodded. "Sure. I'm a fan of the cattle drive as much

as anyone, but the Monarch Festival kicking it off always made us unique. We need to get that back."

"Glad you agree. Like I said, Friday, ten o'clock, out at Fire Gorge Ranch. Seems Mrs. Boone and Widow Lewis are co-chairs for the committee this year."

He stared at her. "You want me to set foot on Woodrow Boone's property? He might shoot first and ask questions later."

"It's an open meeting, advertised to the public. The committee needs people—most committees do. Especially if they're going to try to get this in the works in four weeks' time." Miss Francis eyed his coffee cup. "Helped?"

He grinned, his gaze sweeping the library. No sign of India. A small part of him had hoped she'd listened in, maybe even been a little impressed.

"She's still here," Miss Francis said. "A gentleman would go buy her a coffee." She paused. "Then leave the girl alone. You need to keep your head on straight, Brody Wallace. I've seen the way you look at India, and I'd advise you to wait until the election is over before you start courting her."

"I've no plans to court her," he whispered loudly, vehemently.

Miss Francis rolled her eyes. "I'm old, boy, not blind. I know how long you've been sweet on her and how long you've kept it a secret. All I'm saying is, a few more months won't hurt a thing. I'll see you Friday." She walked away before he could correct her.

He stood there, staring at the bookshelves, racking his brain for a way to set Miss Francis straight. "Damn," he mumbled. Could he? If he were smart, he'd do exactly what she said.

He set out, bought India her coffee and headed back—determined to do just as Miss Francis suggested.

But then he found India in a quiet corner on the floor, propped up against the wall. They'd taken most of the library chairs for his event, and he felt bad she'd been studying on the floor. But with her blond hair falling around her shoulders, and her glasses perched on the end of her nose, all he could think about was sitting on that carpet next to her and finding any excuse to stay.

"Coffee," he said.

She stared up, blinking. "What?"

"Your coffee. Since I stole yours." He held the coffee out, stepping carefully around her sleeping dog to reach her.

She grinned. "I gave it to you. Not exactly stealing." But she took the coffee.

Not gonna sit. Not gonna sit. He sat on the carpet, stretching his long legs out in front of him. "Nice spot."

One fine brow arched. "I normally have actual chairs and a table, but some wannabe important person took them all."

"Wannabe?" He pressed a hand to his chest. "I'd like to think I'm important to someone, somewhere."

She smiled. "I can think of three adorable someones close by who probably think you're the most important person in their world."

He nodded.

"How'd it go?" she asked, nodding at the front of the library.

"Good turnout." He shrugged.

"That's it?" She tucked her pencil behind her ear. "Guess I'll hear about it over breakfast tomorrow."

He froze, pleasure blooming in his chest. "Are we having breakfast tomorrow?"

Her eyes went round. "No. I—I meant my dad…" She swallowed, studying his face. "I didn't mean we'd have breakfast together."

"Why not?" The two words were out before he could stop them. "We're friends after all. And we both need to eat," he added to hide some of his embarrassment.

"Oh." Her forehead furrowed. "I only meant my father reads the paper every morning. It makes for a colorful meal. This morning the vein on his forehead was throbbing, thanks to you."

He sighed. "Not so happy about the announcement?"

She shook her head.

"So I'm guessing breakfast is out, too?" he asked. Why was he pushing this? "I don't want to stir the pot with your father."

She stared at the book in her lap. "I've given up. There's something to be said for knowing you're a disappointment from the get-go. Makes screwing up less of a shock and more of a foregone conclusion." The bite of her words was tempered by her lack of emotion.

"Sounds bleak, India," he murmured. "All I see is a woman determined to be able to provide for herself and her son. That's damn admirable, if you ask me."

"Sorry. I think I just rained on your morning. I didn't mean to. I'm really happy for you—and Fort Kyle, Brody. I know you're going to do good things for this town. I'm glad so many turned out to support you." She paused. "I mean, I didn't hear any hecklers back here, so I'm assuming they were here to support you."

He laughed.

"Where are the girls?" she asked. "There's a reading time at eleven."

He glanced at his watch. "I've got plenty of time to get them and come back." He pushed off the floor. "Since you won't join me for breakfast, maybe you'd think about having lunch with the girls and me? After reading time?"

She glanced from him to her books and back again. He refused to acknowledge her look for the decline it was.

"I'll take that as a maybe," he said. "Keep up the hard work."

She laughed. "I'm trying. But I keep getting interrupted."

"Tell the next person who interrupts you to take a hike."

"Maybe I will," she said, waving and turning back to her books.

He found a small study table and chair and dragged them back to where she sat. "You look uncomfortable," he said, startling her.

"Brody. You didn't have to do that." But she was already putting her things on the table.

"Can't resist. I'm a gentleman, after all." He winked at her.

Her blue-green gaze locked with his, lingering long enough for the air between them to tighten and build. What would she do if he brushed that wayward curl from her cheek? His fingers itched to find out.

"Brody," she managed, clearing her throat.

"Yes?" he asked, resisting the urge to step closer.

"Take a hike." The words were soft, unsteady and dangerously husky.

He smiled. "Sounds good. Tomorrow. After you take Cal to school. I'll meet you here?"

Her eyes went round, and she shook her head. "You are—"

"A genius," he finished. "After all, I just got you to ask me on a hike. I'll let you study now." With another wink, he left her openmouthed and staring after him.

Chapter Five

The next day she was called in to substitute teach a kindergarten class. Mrs. Rios, the regular teacher, had left early the previous day with a stomach flu, and India got to hear all about how poor Mrs. Rios threw up in the hallway after running out of class.

"Mrs. Rios's class is a handful," Cal said as he was getting ready for bed after the end of her second day.

She smiled at her son. "Guess it's a good thing you've got Mrs. Hamilton, then?"

He nodded. "She reads to us lots and has molding clay in her stations all the time—not just for special treats."

India considered Mrs. Hamilton a brave woman. Molding clay, as she'd found out today, could be seriously disruptive in class. Especially when one student decided to fill another student's nose with it. After a quick trip to the school nurse all was well, but those fifteen minutes had her rethinking her career field.

"Mrs. Rios is feeling better, so I think I'll work at the antiques shop," she said as she dried his wet hair. "And then it's the weekend. Anything special you want to do?"

"Find a horse I can ride?" he asked, the hope and anticipation on his face too much to resist. "I can do it, Mom. I just need some practice."

She sighed, running her fingers through his hair. "I

know you can. We'll figure something out, okay? I promise."

He nodded, smiling ear to ear. "Okay." He climbed into bed and pulled his blankets up. "Studying tonight?"

She nodded. She had plenty to do. The problem was she didn't want to do it. No, tonight her restlessness was at an all-time high.

"You get some sleep," she said, stopping to press a kiss to his forehead.

"I will." He yawned around his words, his eyelids already heavy. "I'm beat."

She giggled and stood, turning off his overhead light and flipping on his T. rex night-light. With another, "Night," she pulled his bedroom door shut behind her and leaned against it, staring around the small cabin she and Cal called home. It was a tiny guest cottage on the dude ranch, two bedrooms and a kitchen-dining area. Perched just far enough from the main lodge to give her a sense of independence, its isolation was the reason most guests asked for a different room. And, sometimes, she did feel achingly lonely—though the cabin's location probably didn't have much to do with that.

She pushed through the front door and peered into the black night sky. A million stars sparkled down on her. Between the white rocks cropping up through ground-cover and the light of the moon overhead, the ground was a patchwork quilt of shadow and light.

"India?" Scarlett called out, the beam of a flashlight breaking the pitch-black near the tree line.

"Hey." She waved, relieved by the company.

"I had to escape," Scarlett said, laughing. "Ever since Dad read about Brody, he's all fired up. Mom just told him about the committee meeting tomorrow—"

"She *just* told him? She's been planning it for a month.

Making sure the food and drinks are better than what Mindy-Ellen Shroeder provided when she last hosted the meeting." She shook her head. "I rarely say this, but poor Dad."

Scarlett nodded, climbing up the porch steps. She pulled up the second patio chair and sat. "Yep. On top of the Fort Kyle guests, he has to deal with the county elite."

"Every town in a fifty-mile radius. Poor, poor Dad. It's bound to be long and drawn out. Hobnobbing and small talk and…" She shook her head, laughing.

"You're going to be there, too, right?" Scarlett asked, her smile fading. Her sister didn't do well in crowds.

"Of course. We can team up." India grinned. "I just hope the committee decides to do the right thing. We need the Monarch Festival. No matter how much work it requires."

"Be careful saying that too loudly or you'll be nominated to some action committee. Or put in charge of programming or something." Scarlett drew her feet up and under her. "Sure is quiet out here."

India nodded. "I was just thinking that."

"Sort of a nice change from the main house." Scarlett glanced her way. "How's it going? The studying and the working? And life? And, that thing with Brody?"

India smiled at her sister, who was two years younger. Scarlett was a gentle soul. India worried about her getting lost in the shuffle sometimes. The rest of the family were all loud and stubborn, but not Scarlett. She was the peacemaker. The one who wanted to make everyone happy. Which was impossible. "Good, really. The kids are adorable. It's nice being able to see what Cal's learning and getting to know the kids he goes to school with. Working with Mom and Dad is, as you know, a challenge. And my studies…I just have to keep the goal in mind, you know?"

"I'm tired just listening to you." Scarlett laughed.

"I was feeling a little antsy when you showed up. Must have been your sisterly intuition," India teased.

"I aim to please. What do you have in mind? Hair braiding, polishing each other's nails and boy talk?"

India perked up. "Boy talk? Scarlett Ann Boone, is there a boy we need to talk about?"

Scarlett laughed. "No. I was thinking about you."

"Me? Cal is the only boy in my life."

"I saw you two together, India. And now you're avoiding my question, so I know there's something going on. With Brody Wallace." Scarlett shrugged. "That was the most intense thank-you hug I've ever seen. And Miss Francis sort of implied something might be going on."

India stared. "Are you kidding me?" She knew Miss Francis liked to talk, but there was nothing to tell.

Scarlett shook her head. "I'm not. Are you saying it's not true? I'm sort of bummed."

India didn't know what to say.

Scarlett's sigh echoed in the still of the night. "It's okay if it's true, you know. I've always liked Brody. He's a good guy. And, I promise, I won't say anything to anyone."

"He is a good guy," India agreed. She looked at her sister, tempted to confide her new and alarming reactions to Brody Wallace. She'd forgotten how it felt to have someone on her side. JT hadn't liked her family, and in time, she'd learned to avoid anything that upset him. In hindsight she realized he was cutting her off from the people who'd have stepped in to prevent his ill treatment of her. It had worked. She'd blocked them out—something else her father had yet to forgive her for.

"And?" Scarlett prodded. "India? Go on."

"And we're friends. But…" She swallowed.

Scarlett waited.

"I think I'm lonely. And Brody is…" What was Brody?

"Hot? Sweet? Funny? Awesome?" Scarlett offered. "Ya'll have been *secret pals* for years. Now he could be potential boyfriend material?"

India bit her lip. She was ridiculously attracted to him. Off the charts aware of him. But that didn't mean she needed to do anything about it. Or consider Brody Wallace boyfriend material. "He did buy me a coffee because I gave him mine."

"What about the hug?" Scarlett asked.

"It happened. I hugged him. He hugged me back. We sort of stuck that way." She sighed, savoring the memories of his arms around her and the brush of his breath on her neck. A slight shudder ran down her back. "And I didn't want to let go." She looked at her sister then, nervous and uncertain about sharing like this.

"What's wrong with that, India? Nothing. Nothing at all." Scarlett took her hand. "Just be extra careful. There's not much to do in this town except talk. Now, with the election, a budding romance between a Boone and a Wallace would be the juiciest thing this town has seen in a long time."

India squeezed her hand. Her sister was right. The best plan of action: avoid Brody at all costs. That way she wouldn't have to worry about how he made her react or feel or ache. Or what it would be like for Brody to be more than a friend.

BRODY LINGERED INSIDE the front door of the Fire Gorge Lodge, his hat in his hands, assessing the packed entry hall of the lavish dude ranch. After parking among a sea of custom pickups, BMWs, Mercedes, Audis and the occasional work truck, he knew the key players from the surrounding counties were here, too. But seeing them here in all their finery was a daunting site.

As was the towering image of Woodrow Boone standing at the top of the stairs. He was talking to someone, the smile on his face forced and brittle, and he looked ready to run. A feeling Brody understood but had to ignore if he was going to take his run for mayor seriously. And he was. He hadn't expected the turnout at the library, or his supporters' enthusiasm and willingness to do whatever needed doing. It was just the reaffirmation he needed.

Woodrow Boone's steely gaze locked with his. Hostility rolled off the older man, the tightening of his jaw, the flare of his nostrils and the white-knuckled grip of his hand on the banister. He looked ready to stomp down the stairs and tear into him. But he hesitated, spun on his heel and disappeared from the upstairs landing.

When Brody was joined by Scarlett and Miss Francis, he didn't know. But Scarlett's soft voice pulled him back to the present.

"Hey, Brody, glad you made it," Scarlett said.

"And found parking," Miss Francis added. "We're all packed in like sardines."

"Means no one is leaving," Brody said, putting on his best smile. "A captive audience. Might be useful if everyone's set against revitalizing the Monarch Festival."

"It's a mixed reaction," Scarlett said. "But I think a firm nudge in the right direction—"

"A couple of your megawatt, charming smiles can't hurt." Miss Francis nudged him in the side.

Scarlett giggled. "Well, I don't think it will take much to remind them how important the festival is to the community."

"Surely local businesses have seen it affect their bottom line?" Brody asked.

"It's been two years." Miss Francis shook her head. "It'll take more than that before they start to feel it in their pocketbook."

"And by then the tradition of the festival will be a memory." Brody sighed.

"That's why you're here," Scarlett said, smiling.

"That, and making your father see red." He glanced at the landing, but there was no sign of Mr. Woodrow Boone.

"Already?" Scarlett asked.

"Hey, Brody." Cal ran up, all smiles and childhood enthusiasm. "Like your boots. Got some new ones myself." He held up his foot, tugging up his jeans so Brody could inspect them.

His only choice was dropping to a knee to do just that. "Soft leather. Good fit. And the tooling—nice details."

Cal nodded. "Got 'em this morning."

"I approve," he said, tugging Cal's pants leg down before standing and patting the boy's shoulder. And coming face-to-face with India. Her smile was so sweet it made his chest ache.

"Hi. You're here," she murmured, her gaze darting nervously around the room. He couldn't tell if she was happy to see him or not. "Have you seen my dad? Mom wants him."

"He's upstairs." He smiled at her. "He wasn't happy to see me. Took one look at me and disappeared."

India blew out a long, slow breath, her gaze searching his.

"I knew coming out here wasn't a good idea—"

"He's just being…Dad," Scarlett argued. "Of course you're welcome."

"It's a public meeting, Brody," India said. "Anyone with an opinion on the fate of the Monarch Festival is invited—especially mayoral candidates."

"I'm pretty sure that's part of the problem." Brody laughed.

Glancing at the stairs, India said, "Come on, Cal, let's go drag your grandfather from his study and make him be social."

Cal's shoulders slumped. "His study is off-limits."

"Not today. He can bluster and complain all he wants." India took Cal's hand in hers. "He never says no to your grandma."

"I'll come, too," Scarlett offered.

Brody watched the three of them ascend the stairs, the women each holding one of Cal's hands. The boy was smiling by the time they reached the top of the stairs, his gaze bouncing back and forth between his mother and his aunt.

"Maybe you should have brought your girls," Miss Francis said. "The man has daughters—he's sure to have a soft spot for them. And they are precious girls."

"That's just what I need right now. Chasing after Amberleigh with her clothes in one hand and her shoes in the other," he argued.

Miss Francis laughed then. "Maybe you're right. She'll grow out of it soon enough, don't you worry. No sense standing around out here. Let's go shake some hands, mingle and show you off."

"You clean up well, Miss Francis," he said, leading them into an open meeting room outfitted with a bar and a few tables and chairs.

"I don't mind getting dressed up when necessary," she said, patting his arm.

He grinned. Whatever she was wearing, the old

woman had a commanding presence that earned her attention and respect from all who met her. And Brody admired the hell out of her.

"Where do we start?" he asked.

"Why, with Mayor Draper, of course," she murmured. "I saw him earlier. Now's as good a time as any to be cordial and neighborly. You know, keep this election civil and all."

He hoped she was right. He had nothing but respect for the man who had served Fort Kyle so long.

"Brody Wallace," the old man wheezed as they approached, extending an unsteady hand. "Nice to see you out and about, boy."

Brody swallowed his surprise and took the man's hand. "You, too, sir."

"I hear you're going to finally replace me?" Mayor Draper asked. "I kept waiting for someone to run, someone to step up and take the reins. 'Bout time. I'm tired," he said, clapping Brody's shoulder with his other hand. "And I'm mighty glad it's you."

When Brody had imagined this meeting, this was a scenario that had never crossed his mind. He would run unchallenged? He was aware of their growing audience. If they were looking for drama, they'd be disappointed. "That means a lot, sir. I have some mighty big shoes to fill, but I give you my word I'll work hard to do the best I can for our fine town and the people who live hereabouts."

Mayor Draper nodded and released his hand. "I believe you will, son. I believe you will."

"Good intentions or not, it won't be easy." Woodrow Boone joined them, doing his damnedest not to look Brody in the eye. "You've been doing a fine job, John.

You can't just step aside without giving the people a vote. I'm not so sure Fort Kyle is ready to see you go."

John Draper snorted. "I think I've earned the right to make my own mind up on this one, Woodrow. It won't be easy, that's the truth. But he's young, eager, with brains to boot. He'll do fine. More than fine, I reckon." He grinned, his cloudy eyes glancing between the two of them. "But we're not here to talk politics today, are we? We're here to talk about the Monarch Festival."

Brody appreciated Draper's seamless shift in conversation. Intentional or not, John Draper kept the tension compressed and the focus where it needed to be: Fort Kyle's economic future.

In ten minutes, everyone was ushered into the dining room for a buffet brunch complete with fancy china and instrumental classic country tunes piped in through the speakers. Brody took his time exploring. In all his years, he'd been invited here only twice, not including today. But both his prom and his senior-year awards banquet were hazy now. His prom had consisted of dancing with every girl besides India, while being aware of her every movement. She'd looked so damn pretty in her pink dress, he'd had a hard time keeping his distance—even with Mrs. Boone serving as chaperone.

His senior awards banquet had been overshadowed by the huge fight he'd had with his parents. No matter how much he and his mother had pleaded and explained how important the awards were, his father flat-out refused to set foot on Boone property. Eventually he'd gone on his own, red-faced and stiff through most of the evening. While his peers had their friends and family to cheer them on, he sat alone. India had shot him sympathetic glances throughout the evening, but her parents' attendance had prevented her from being at his side.

Everything about Fire Gorge Lodge was impressive. From the outside, it appeared to be one massive log cabin. But inside, it was pure elegance—with a dash of rustic thrown in for atmosphere. Sure, there were antlers and hunting trophies on the walls, pictures of generations of Boones working the ranch as well as faded tintype photos of the Boone ancestors. The pride in their heritage was obvious. But the attention to the comfort of guests who frequented the dude ranch—overstuffed chairs, massive televisions, technology-charging stations, arctic air-conditioning—made it clear they understood their clientele's expectations.

"Like what you see?" Woodrow Boone asked, his tone hard and cold.

"I do, sir. It's an impressive setup." He looked the man squarely in the eye, determined not to let the man intimidate him. "It was mighty generous of you to host this meeting—"

"My wife's idea." He scowled. "I'd have been far more selective with the invitations."

Brody pressed his lips tight. His only response was a nod.

"Why are you here?" the man asked, stepping closer. The words bordered on a growl, low and deep and menacing. "So you can get your picture in the paper again and shake hands with the real royalty hereabouts? Or because you know there's no way I can kick your ass off my property without making a scene?"

Brody winced at Woodrow Boone's bluntness. He'd hoped there was a chance of civility between them—Brody wasn't his father. "I wanted to offer my help and support for revitalizing the Monarch Festival. I meant you no personal offense—"

"No?" Woodrow Boone's face was turning an alarming shade of red. "You really thought I wouldn't be offended by a Wallace—a name that has slandered mine loudly and publicly—taking advantage of the comforts of my home?"

From the corner of his eye he saw India practically running their way. "Daddy." She slid her arm through Woodrow's, tugging him back. "You promised Mom."

"I don't need *you* reminding me to keep my promises," he barked, shaking off her touch.

Brody saw the hurt on her face and ached for her. Whatever point the man had been trying to make with his comment, his words had hit their mark.

India's cheeks blazed red, her gaze shifting from her father to the dining room doors. "Lunch is being served."

"I'll be along when I'm good and ready," Woodrow countered, his voice noticeably rising. "I don't need you handling me, India. And I don't like you trying."

India stared at the floor, but her tone was urgent. "Dad, please, we have guests. And Mom—"

"I'm behaving," Woodrow snapped, his irritation easing. "Mr. Wallace, here, needs to understand when his dessert plate is cleared, his time is up. After that, he is no longer welcome on this property." His smile was hard. "Ever." He waited for Brody's nod before marching into the dining room.

The man was a bastard. Brody didn't give a shit about the way Woodrow talked to him. But India? He'd no cause to talk down to her like that. It got his blood boiling. "You okay?" he asked.

Her green-blue eyes met his. "Me?"

"Chaps my hide to hear him talk to you like that. I can't imagine talking to the girls that way, no matter how caught up in anger I was." His hands fisted at his side.

"You're a good father, Brody. Your girls are lucky to have you." The longing in her voice was hard to miss.

"Damn shame," he grumbled, happy to have her close. He could study the curve of her cheek, the long sweep of her lashes and the slight scar slicing through her left eyebrow. He didn't know that scar—and he'd known every inch of her face well.

Her gaze met his. "That went better than I expected." Her smile eased the hard knot pressing against his chest.

"It did?" he asked, itching to touch her.

"I fully expected him to come downstairs carrying Martha," India said, tugging him toward the dining room.

"Martha?" Brody asked, his concern over Woodrow fading at the sweet smile India sent over his shoulder.

"Dad's favorite pistol." India stopped, her gaze sweeping over him. "You're lucky he promised Mom he'd behave, or things could have taken a turn for the worse."

He stared at her, stunned.

"Go dazzle the crowd. And bring back the Monarch Festival." She patted his chest and disappeared into the dining room. She was teasing him. She'd always loved teasing him. Surely, she was joking about the gun. A quick glance at Woodrow Boone and he wasn't so sure.

One thing he was absolutely certain of—the way India made him feel. Standing there, staring after her, he didn't care about her father, the election or the crowds of people he was supposed to "charm." All he wanted was time alone with her.

He walked up to the lodge's reception desk and asked the clerk to borrow a pen and paper. Then he wrote,

"Full moon tonight. Going to the ridge for some peace and quiet. Hope you'll join me." He folded the note, tucked it into an envelope and put her name on it. "Can you make sure India Boone gets this?" he asked the clerk. "Nobody else."

Chapter Six

"And then they traveled to all the fairy castles, gnome mushroom villages and mermaid coves, spreading joy and friendship wherever they went." Brody closed the book. "The end. Everyone into her own bed. It's late." For them. He loved their bedtime routine, but he was worn out and ready for some quiet. He had plans tonight—he hoped.

Today had been productive.

First, the Monarch Festival was going to happen. Once a handful of local businesses put up the majority of the money, plenty of folks offered up their time and talents. From the Butterfly Kissing Booth, face painting and butterfly crafts to butterfly cakes and treats—this promised to be the biggest festival yet.

Second, unless someone else jumped in at the last minute, he'd soon be mayor of Fort Kyle.

Lastly, India preoccupied far too much of his mind. And it wasn't just because she was the most mesmerizing thing he'd ever set eyes on. She was beautiful, yes, but she was also sad. And he couldn't bear to watch. Even sitting across the dining room, he could see it. That was why he'd left her a note asking her to meet him at the ridge. That was why he needed the girls to go to bed without a fight.

Was it a damn foolish move? Yes. He knew one night of stargazing on the ridge wouldn't make her happy. Was it likely to backfire? Definitely. Damn it all, he loved her, there was no way around it. All he knew was she needed someone. And he wanted to be that someone. Whatever she needed, whatever she wanted—he'd do his best to give it to her. He might regret it once she'd left town… but he was doing it anyway.

He turned to his girls. "You three princesses have sweet dreams. All about cookies and cupcakes, and dragon eggs, too." He added the last with a wink for Amberleigh.

"Daddy?" Marilyn asked. "Drink, please."

"Me, too?" Suellen asked, sliding from her bed. "I'll help."

Brody sighed but let Suellen help him get three glasses of water. It was a production. Marilyn needed pink, Suellen blue and Amberleigh dragon green. He filled their cups, put them on a tray and carried them back to their room—Suellen trailing behind him. She distributed their cups, taking teeny-tiny steps so she wouldn't spill.

"Not thirsty," Amberleigh said.

"You might get thirsty later," Brody said, watching Suellen set Amberleigh's green cup down with the utmost care.

"Daddy?" Suellen asked, climbing into bed again. "Dragons come from eggs? Like chickens?"

He looked at Amberleigh. "I *think* so."

Amberleigh nodded.

"Eggs make babies. Cute babies." Suellen laughed.

He chuckled.

"No." Amberleigh frowned, making claw hands. "Dragons *scary.*"

Marilyn moaned. "No scary dreams." She sniffed, her big eyes welling up with tears.

"Daddy, no," Suellen wailed. "No scary dreams."

Amberleigh's eyelids drifted shut.

"No, no, now, your dream dragons will protect you," he assured them, hoping he sounded convincing. "They keep all princesses safe and sound and watch over them when they sleep."

"They do?" Marilyn asked, wiping a tear away with the back of her hand.

"Sure," he said, out of his element. He wasn't raised on make-believe and fairy tales. But seeing his girls in tears was too much for him. "I'll bring Lollipop in here, too. He'll come get me or Nana or Granddad. Okay?" He leaned out the door. "Lollipop, come on." He patted his leg, watching the tiny dog barrel down the hall— a white fluffy flash that leaped up onto Amberleigh's bed. "Better?"

Suellen nodded. Marilyn sniffed but nodded, too. Amberleigh was already sleeping, completely unaware of Lollipop nudging beneath her arm and burrowing close to her sleeping form. He turned on their princess crown night-light and flipped off the overhead. "You girls sleep sweet. Tomorrow we'll go shopping for your birthday party next month."

"Gonna be three," Suellen said, holding up three fingers.

"Go to school?" Marilyn asked.

"I'll check. We can ask Cal's momma. She teaches at the school."

"Ask, Daddy," Suellen said.

"I'll go do that," he said. "You get some sleep and we'll talk about school at breakfast tomorrow morning. Night, girls. Sleep tight."

"Night," they said in unison before he pulled the door around, leaving it cracked behind him.

He lingered in the hall. Experience had taught him to stay put for at least five minutes. The girls tended to slip out of bed and wander, wanting more water, another kiss or a bathroom visit before he had to tuck them in again. If he caught them early on, he could stop the dawdling and stall tactics.

"How'd it go today?" his father asked when he walked into the living room. His dad was working on his nightly crossword puzzle while his mother sat in her recliner, knitting needles furiously clicking. "I still can't believe you went *there*."

"Vic." The needles stopped clicking. "Your blood pressure."

"It went well. The county really rallied—ready and willing to make the Monarch Festival happen." He leaned against the arched doorway. "And Mayor Draper is stepping aside."

His mother smiled. "Congratulations, sweetie."

"Mayor Wallace." His father smiled, peering over his black reading glasses.

He smiled back. "Overall a good day."

His father sat back, watching him closely. "You see him?"

The knitting needles stopped again. "Of course he did, he lives there. Honestly, Vic, sometimes I think you want him to pick a fight."

His father scowled at his mother. "That's ridiculous, Ramona. I just know Woodrow Boone. Hotheaded, inflated and downright nasty. Having a Wallace under his roof must have—"

"We kept our distance," Brody interrupted, hoping to keep his parents calm. He wasn't a fan of Woodrow

Boone either, but he knew his father had done more than his fair share to make the other man that way.

"Huh," he said, almost disappointed. "Well, there it is." His father shook his head and leaned over his crossword again.

"You going out?" his mother asked, her keen gaze sweeping over him. "You look nice."

"For a bit, if that's all right?" he asked. "The girls are in bed for the night."

"You go on," his mother said. "We'll call if we need you."

With a smile and a nod he left, climbed into his truck and took the winding back roads that led to the ridge. The farther he drove, the darker it grew. He might have spent a few years away, but he knew this land—blindfolded. If he didn't, he'd be at risk of driving off the edge of the rocky cliff ravine that gave Fire Gorge its name.

He slowed when he reached the summit, a perfectly flat surface that made this place perfect for stargazing. He turned, backed closer to the edge of the ridge and parked. As soon as he turned off his headlights, he was consumed by darkness. He let his eyes adjust before he climbed out of his cab. A steady breeze held the slightest hint of a chill and a welcome relief.

He sucked in a deep breath and opened his back door, released the seat and tugged his emergency sleeping bags out. He'd been caught out in an ice storm once, a blown axle and miles from help, without a thing to warm him up. Now he kept two sleeping bags, water and some trail mix stored behind his seat. Perfect for sitting and solving the world's problems—or sharing burdens.

If India decided to show up.

INDIA DROVE SLOWLY along the rutted dirt road. *What am I doing?* Her hands tightened on the steering wheel. Driving in pitch-dark, along a sheer drop, to meet a man who stirred up far too many distracting wants and emotions. But his note had tugged at the loneliness deep inside.

Full moon tonight. Going to the ridge for some peace and quiet. Hope you'll join me.

She should have spoken to Scarlett before leaving. It had been so nice to catch up and reconnect with her, to share and be a little vulnerable. Scarlett had agreed to watch Cal, but India hadn't said where she was going. Letting someone in wasn't easy for her—sister or no.

So why am I driving to the middle of nowhere to meet a man—

A blur of movement exploded out of the dark, streaking from the right and cutting across the truck's path. Her brain shut off, unleashing panic and reacting without thought—instinct had her jerking the steering wheel sharply to the right. The dirt and rocks of the road provided no resistance. The truck spun once and again, bouncing off the road, tipping forward, slamming into the side ditch and coming to an abrupt stop.

She sat still, stunned and sore from the bite of the seat belt. The truck was wedged at an angle. While her seat belt kept her locked in place, the cab and hood of the truck sat at a severe downward slant. She turned the engine over and put it into Drive, but the car didn't move. Reverse was no better. It was stuck. She was stuck.

"Perfect," she ground out, resting her head on the truck headrest. She couldn't walk out of here at this time of night. West Texas was home to mountain lions, bobcats, javelinas, snakes and the occasional black bear—all beautiful, majestic creatures she had no interest in encountering in the wild.

She flipped on the interior lights, wincing from the bright white flooding the cabin. Her purse had slid across the seat and spilled its contents all over the floor of the cab. Including her phone. If she was lucky she'd be able to call Scarlett. But the seat belt buckle wouldn't release, and even stretching, she couldn't reach it.

"Damn it," she ground out. She stared out the window into the darkness.

Lights were coming. They stretched along, growing larger as whatever vehicle bounced along the road. Flying down the road. She honked, waited a few seconds and honked again. "Please, please…" she whispered.

It was Brody. When his red truck pulled alongside the ditch, relief slammed into her so hard she almost burst into tears. Almost.

"India?" he called, jumping from the cab as soon as the vehicle came to a stop. "India? You okay?"

"I'm fine," she answered, pushing the driver door wide. "My seat belt's stuck, though."

Brody straddled the ditch between her truck and the road, trying the buckle release. "Might want to brace yourself," he said, pulling his pocketknife from his pocket.

She held on to the seat back with one hand and pushed against the dashboard with the other while he cut through the strap. It was the wrong time to notice how good he smelled. Or how nice his hands felt holding hers, helping her out of the truck and onto the road. One hand smoothed the hair from her forehead while the other tilted her face up. "I saw your lights spinning like crazy and got here as fast as I could. What the hell happened? Are you okay?"

"I'm fine. Something ran out in front of me. I swerved." She shook her head, leaning against him. Her heart was still thumping, and her nerves were shot. But having his arms slide around her was nice. So was his scent. Her toes curled in her boots, her fingers plucking at his shirt. His scent wasn't just nice. She breathed deeply—nervousness and fear forgotten.

"Damn lucky you swerved right and not left." His hand rubbed up and down her back. "Damn lucky." His voice was soft, his voice a husky whisper at her ear.

"For me, yes." She drew in a wavering breath. He was right. Tonight could have taken a turn for the worse—if she'd gone left she'd likely be at the bottom of the ridge. She shuddered. Right now, she was very thankful to be alive. And pressed tight against him. She might be enjoying that part a little too much.

"You're okay?" he murmured, holding her away from him so he could inspect her.

The truck chose that moment to make an odd hiss-pop sound. She wasn't mechanical, but that couldn't be good. "But not the truck." The truck was the only thing she owned free and clear, and she needed it. How was she going to get to work? Or Cal to school? She already relied too heavily on her parents. Now she was going to have to borrow a Fire Gorge work truck. "Maybe it's not that bad?" Even she heard the doubt in her voice.

"It's too dark to tell how bad the damage is. I'll come out first thing in the morning, see if I can use a chain to pull it out or if it'll need the tractor." He grinned. "Either way, I'll get it out and see if my friend Danny can fix it quick."

Her problem wasn't his responsibility. She didn't want to be indebted to anyone but… "I should argue with you and try to stop you."

"Why?" His brow furrowed.

Why indeed. Brody wasn't the type to hold things over her. He wasn't her ex-husband or her father. He was *Brody.* She shook her head.

"Come on, India," he sighed. "This is a no-strings, no-stress offer here, okay?"

How could she argue with that? "Thank you, really. When you have an idea of the repairs, let me know... Or the cost." She mumbled the last part. Repairs were going to take a solid chunk of her precious savings. And delay her plans. Not to mention, cause a headache with her dad when she borrowed a vehicle.

"I never should have suggested meeting out here like this." There was guilt in his voice—something he had no right to feel.

He was worrying over her, trying to take care of her *and* her vehicle, for crying out loud. She was not about to let him feel guilty over any of this. "I didn't have to come, you know." She nudged him, for good measure.

His gaze met hers. "But you did." He sounded...*happy*.

She nodded, an odd tightness weighing down her chest. Something about the way he was looking at her made the truck, the potential repair bills, even her uncertainty about this evening melt away. All that remained was a longing so fierce she could scarcely breathe. "I did," she whispered.

"What do we do now?" he asked.

What indeed. She knew what she didn't want to do. Leave. "Well... We're here. If there's nothing we can do about the truck tonight—" She pointed at the truck.

"Not tonight," he agreed, smiling.

"Maybe we don't need to rush home?" Why was she nervous about his answer?

"Not when there's a full moon out. Like you said, we're here and all."

She smiled. "Exactly."

"Need anything out of there?" he asked.

"My purse sort of exploded." She grinned.

"Give me a sec," he said, hopping from the road to the truck and leaning in.

A noise off the side of the road made the hair on the back of her neck stand up. "Brody?" she called out.

"What's up?" he called back.

"There's something out here." She moved closer to his truck, standing in the beam of his truck headlights.

"Hold up," he said, emerging from her truck with her purse in hand. He moved with surprising grace back to her side and held out her brown leather purse. "Think I got it all."

"Thanks." She gripped the bag close.

He spun around, peering into the dark. "Probably feral pigs. Dad thought it was javelinas, so I set up a game camera—to see their comings and goings. Damn sons-o-bitches have made short work of our back-pasture fences and damaged two of the water tanks." His fingers threaded with hers as he led her to his truck. "Probably caused less damage to your truck swerving than hitting 'em. Got a picture of the pack. The male was big. Probably weighed between three and four hundred pounds."

Her father had mentioned them a few weeks back. They'd had a sighting on one of their trail rides and decided to reroute the ride to be safe.

"Are they dangerous?" she asked, glancing over her shoulder.

"Can be. But they'd rather run than fight." He opened his passenger door. "Still, I'd rather not stick around to chance it." He winked and slammed the door.

She watched him walk around the hood of the truck. He was searching the dark—alert and ready. When he climbed into the cab beside her, she let out a long, low breath and relaxed.

He must have heard her. "You okay?" he asked, glancing at her in the dimly lit cab.

She nodded. "Better now."

"Not feeling adventurous this evening?" He chuckled.

She rolled her eyes. "I've never been adventurous, Brody."

"That is a lie." He shook his head. "I went to school with you, remember? Sneaking toads into that mean ol' substitute teacher's purse. Punching Johnny Gill in the throat for cutting off your sister's pigtail. Oh, and there was that little incident with the vapor rub in a certain athlete's cup."

She grinned. "All deserved. I was young. I'm a much more…grounded adult." She laughed. "Being adventurous is part of being young, don't you think?"

He was grinning. "I guess it is."

"For a minute I forgot who I was talking to." She turned in her seat. "You are running for mayor, Brody Wallace. I'd say that's pretty adventurous."

He nodded. "Maybe a little."

"A little? I hope you know what you're getting yourself into." She shook her hair free from the drooping bun at the back of her head, then started twisting it up again.

"What am I getting myself into?" he asked, glancing her way.

"My father, for one." She tried to secure her hair, but the hairclip slipped from her fingers and fell to the floorboard.

"Your hair is pretty, India. Leave it down." The words were low and deep, making the air between them hum. "If you like." A charged silence filled the truck.

When he parked, he turned to face her. "Speaking of your father."

"We don't have to—"

"I'd say it's pretty adventurous to sneak out in the middle of the night to meet me. Considering how fond he is of me and my family." He grinned.

"We're a little old to be asking for approval on who we can and can't be friends with." She looked at him, and he was looking at her. Instead of getting lost in his gaze, she studied the line of his jaw and the angles of his face. He had a handsome face—a good face.

She'd never reacted this way to him before. But now, there was a spark here. It was real and potent, flooding the space between them and drawing them closer. And she was curious to see where this could go.

That was one of the reasons she was here. For his friendship, yes. His great sense of humor, too. But she'd be lying if this new push-and-pull between them hadn't also factored into it. It had, far too much.

Brody cleared his throat and slipped from the cab, walking around to open her door. She smiled, stepped down and stumbled—falling out the door and into his arms. She gripped his shirtfront, steadying herself and holding on.

His heart pounded beneath her hand. His hands stayed at her waist long after they needed to. But she didn't mind. He was shaking, ever so slightly. And his breath was unsteady. It eased her to think she wasn't the only one struggling with this new awareness. If that was why he was reacting this way.

There was only one way to know. She really wanted to know. Shoving all doubts and fears and logical arguments aside was easy, and so was sliding her arms around his neck. He was tall, tall enough that she was on her tiptoes. But that was okay—he had her. She welcomed the strength and support of his arms around her. And the slight hitch in his breath as he bent his head toward hers. She didn't know if he kissed her or she kissed him—it didn't matter.

His lips were firm. His hands were strong. And she held on for dear life.

Chapter Seven

She was lost in the taste of Brody's lips and the sweet urgency of his hands. This was how a man should kiss. This was how she wanted to feel. Breathless and alive and vital. When his lips had parted hers, his tongue had short-circuited her brain, wiping thoughts of the rest of the world firmly from her mind. Just the feel of him. His scent. His strength. He pressed her against the truck, twined his fingers in her hair and kissed her until his arms were the only thing keeping her upright.

"It's raining." His whisper was part growl, tightening the knot of anticipation low down in her stomach.

Who cared about rain? She didn't. "Let it rain," she said, eager for more of this—more of Brody. She tugged his shirt from his jeans, a soft moan slipping from her lips at the way his skin contracted under her fingertip, the hitch in his breathing. Her touch did that to him, and she loved it.

His kiss deepened, a sort of desperate urgency sweeping them away. The ache was raw and consuming. Each touch, each kiss only made it more so. The muscles of his back shifted as his hands slid up her sides. The rasp of his stubble against her cheek. The twist of his fingers in her hair. He cradled her close, fiercely, tenderly, like she was something precious. This was something she'd never had before—and it had her reeling.

A clap of thunder signaled the beginning. And the end. The skies opened up, dropping gallons of water in a matter of seconds and pulling them apart.

"Damn," he ground out against her lips. "We've got to go."

She was vaguely aware of getting into his truck and the drive back to Fire Gorge. What did this mean? What had happened? She'd been attracted to other men before. Dated a few. But nothing this...intense. This primal. If he hadn't said something, she'd still be holding on to him—in the pouring rain. Once his lips met hers, letting go hadn't entered her mind. One glance his way told her he was equally as stunned by what had passed between them. But neither of them said a word.

She had to say something. Anything. He couldn't leave now. Not with *this* hanging between them.

He pulled up in front of her cabin, and Scarlett came out onto the front porch, an umbrella in hand. But her sister's eyes went round, and she slipped back inside the cabin.

She looked at him then, the fire in his gaze making her heart kick into overdrive. "Brody..." She blew out a deep breath. "I guess we have a lot to talk about."

He grinned. "I'd say so."

But sitting there, with the rain bouncing off the truck with increasing power, wasn't the right time. She didn't want him driving once the roads started flooding. "Tomorrow?" India moved to open the door, but Brody's hand stopped her.

His fingers threaded with hers, lifting her hand to his lips. "I don't know what that was, but I liked it. I just don't want it messing us up. Okay?"

He liked it? She was still on fire, wanting him so. Watching him press his lips against her knuckles made her shiver. She didn't want to lose his friendship. But she did want this man, desperately.

"India?" His voice was gruff. And tempting.

"Yes. No. I know…" She tugged her hand free, got out of the truck and ran through the rain to her front door. If she stayed in that cab a minute longer, everything would change. She would have reached for him and he wouldn't have stopped her, and talking would have been the last thing on either of their minds.

"You're all wild-eyed and out of breath." Scarlett took one look at her soaking clothes and said, "You go shower and clean up."

"Okay," she managed, pausing. "My truck… It's stuck in a rut out on the ridge. Tomorrow…"

"I'll drive you. Glad you're okay," she said. "Now go warm up. You're making me cold just looking at you."

India nodded and headed to the bathroom, not the least bit cold. Nope, the fire Brody had lit was still burning hot on the inside. She took a short shower, hoping to get Scarlett's opinion—to see if this was as crazy as it seemed. But her sister was gone, a mug of hot chocolate on her table and a sweet note, "Sleep tight, see you in the morning, xoxo—Scarlett."

She climbed into bed, but sleep eluded her. If that kiss was any indication of what would come next… Her hands fisted in her sheets. Yes, she was crazy to even consider a next. He was Brody, her friend, one of her only friends. This made no sense. And it could cost her someone she cared a great deal about. But, the things he'd made her feel… Even as she finally drifted to sleep, her mind was bouncing back and forth between what could be and why it should—or shouldn't—happen.

The morning was black and stormy, and the alarm didn't go off. She and Cal scrambled to get ready before Scarlett came to pick them up. Cal chattered all the way to school, which was good since India knew Scarlett would have questions. Once he was dropped off, Scarlett headed to the antiques shop, Tanner resting his big head on the seat back between them.

"Looks like Mom is already here." Scarlett sighed. "I was going to get coffee and some pastries and come back and get the scoop, but I guess that will wait."

India sighed. "I could really use your advice."

"My advice? You know I've never had a boyfriend, India. I might not be the best person to talk to about this."

India looked at her sister. She'd never had a boyfriend? How did India not know this?

"I know, it's sad, but you have to admit the pickings are slim." She shook her head. "Besides, I'd much rather hear about your actual love life than talk about my non-existent one." Scarlett giggled.

"I'll see you after work? Or I'll text you when Mom leaves?"

"Sounds good." Scarlett nodded. "I'll bring coffee or something hot."

With a smile and a wave, she ran through the rain and into the shop.

The rain kept customers away and sent her mother into an organizational tirade. But the entire time she was inventorying dusty odds and ends and listening to her mother's endless complaining about her father's mood since Brody announced his run for mayor, India was thinking about Brody. And an idea was beginning to take shape. A scandalous, ridiculous idea she wasn't sure she'd have the nerve to put into actual words, but it was one of two options.

One, forget last night ever happened. Or two, engage in a no-strings fling with the man she was crazily attracted to. As long as the no-strings part of it was understood and assured and no harm would come to their friendship.

Which sounded absurd. How could she go to bed with Brody and stay friends? Was that possible? The bigger question was, could they engage in this without involving their families? The last thing she needed was her dad finding out—she was a grown woman but she was dependent on him right now, and while she hated indulging in the feud drama, she also couldn't disrespect her dad when he'd opened his home to her and Cal. Besides, her cabin on the ranch might not be permanent, but it also wasn't guaranteed. Cal and the triplets were another concern. The kids couldn't get attached—she'd be leaving Fort Kyle as soon as she was able.

She and Brody were adults. If they went into this with no illusions, it could be good. Or great. She fully expected it to be great. There was no denying the fact that they shared a mutual attraction. Why not act on it—pure attraction?

"I'm heading out. You need anything?" her mother asked, her umbrella in hand. "Since it's slow, with the weather and all. If you want to close up shop after school lets out, that's fine by me."

"Thanks, Mom," she said, tapping her pen against the tablet she'd been doodling on.

"You okay, India? You've been awful lost in your thoughts today. I'm worried you're working too hard. It's not good for you. Maybe you could join the quilting circle? Or the book club? Something you'd enjoy that's just for enjoyment's sake." Her mother paused. "There's nothing wrong with having a little fun now and then."

If only her mother knew what sort of fun she'd been thinking about for most of the day. "I'll try, Mom. You be careful driving in this weather."

Her mother smiled. "I will. You, too. Dad sent in a work truck to get you home." She'd told her parents about the feral pig, but not where she'd been going at the time. "I'll see you later on at Fire Gorge." Her mother pushed through the front door, opened her umbrella and hurried up the near-flooded street toward her Cadillac SUV.

India set her pen down and walked toward the front windows. The taillights of her mother's vehicle disappeared at the end of Main Street. A quick look told her most of the street was deserted.

Because of the rain. She could remember just how it felt against her cheeks, with Brody's lips pressed against hers. Even now, standing in her mother's shop, she felt warm. And alive.

The phone rang, so she hurried back to the counter. "Antiques and Treasures on Main Street. How can I help you?"

"India? Katherine McGee. I wanted to touch base with you about the Monarch Festival. I saw you signed up to volunteer. Did you have something in mind?"

Saying no to volunteering? "No—"

"We're only asking folks to work two-hour shifts, so they won't miss out on the fun. Since you've helped make wings before, would you mind helping with that? It's nice when we have someone with experience for that one—since it can be messy."

India had made a new set of wings every festival. Wire clothes hangers, wrapping paper rolls, pipe cleaners, tissue paper, old sheets and more. Whatever she could get her hands on, she'd use. For a girl with a good imagination, and a solid coating of glitter, anything could be turned into butterfly wings. "For one shift?"

"And, maybe, we could ask you to work the Butterfly Kissing Booth. You're young and pretty and might entice a few more fellas over for a kiss or two." The woman laughed.

India frowned. "Mrs. McGee, I'm not sure I'm the right woman for the job—"

"Nonsense, India. You're gorgeous. And sweet. Butterfly kisses aren't real kisses—eyelashes instead of lips. Maybe even have some real fun and buy yourself some false eyelashes to really tickle."

A clap of thunder shook the front windows, drawing India's gaze. A red truck was parking in front of the shop. Brody's red truck.

"How does that sound?" Mrs. McGee asked.

She was only half listening now. He was here. And her idea no longer seemed like a bad idea. It seemed ridiculous. And yet, for the first time in her adult life, she wanted to be adventurous. With Brody Wallace. "Fine," she mumbled.

"Oh good, good. India, I so appreciate this—we all do."

India watched as Brody ran through the rain onto the covered wood porch and opened the door to the shop. He stood inside, his jacket dripping on the welcome mat covering the wooden floor of the old building.

"I'm happy to help," India murmured. One more distraction she didn't need.

Brody winked at her and hung his coat on the coat rack and his hat on the hook above that.

He was gorgeous. His tight jeans hugged his thighs and showcased his rear to perfection. When he crossed the room and leaned against the counter at her side, all she could do was stare.

"This year's festival promises to be the best so far," Mrs. McGee said.

India hurriedly jotted down the dates and times Mrs. McGee gave her for the next meetings and said her good-byes. She hung up the rotary phone handset, tried to calm the nervous tingles in her stomach and smiled up at Brody.

"Afternoon," he said, his eyes searching hers. "Almost had to charter a boat to get into town."

"Hope you didn't go through all that trouble on my account." Why did her voice sound like that? Tight and high and girlish. She cleared her throat.

He shrugged. "Don't have your cell number. Figured calling here or your place and risking someone else answering might not go over well."

She shook her head, wrote her number on a slip of paper and handed it to him. "Here. You think no one noticed your coming in here?" Half of Fort Kyle lived with their binoculars in one hand and their phones in the other. Then again, the rain had things closed up tight for the most part.

He chuckled, tucking the paper into his coat pocket. "Maybe I'm looking for something for my girls' birthday?"

His scent reached her—stirring up every vivid second of last night. She breathed deep and leaned against the counter. "Are you?"

"No," he admitted, his gaze locking with hers. "But it's a good cover story."

She pushed off the counter, putting space between them before she did something foolish. Like kiss him.

"Couldn't get to your truck." He followed her, his gaze

steady on her as she straightened a knickknack, smoothed a wrinkle from an old quilt draped on a hanging rack and arranged a handful of worn books on the shelf.

She shook her head. "I was worried you'd try to go out there. The road always washes out so—"

"You were worried about me?" he asked, following her.

She took an awkward step-hop back. "Of course. I mean—I couldn't live with myself if something happened to you. Your daughters probably wouldn't think too highly of me, either."

His eyes narrowed a little, the muscle in his jaw tightening. "You look tired."

She hadn't slept much. Because of him.

"Didn't get much sleep?" he asked, picking up an old brass popcorn popper.

"No," she admitted, her voice low and husky.

"Me neither," he said, placing the popcorn popper back on the shelf.

"Oh?" she asked, her lungs emptying as he closed the distance between them.

"Not a wink." His gaze traveled slowly over her face. "My mind wouldn't shut off. All night long. Spinning." He shook his head. "Last night." He broke off with a slight shake of his head.

She sucked in a deep breath, but it didn't help. He was so close she couldn't escape the effect he had on her. Last night had lit a fire inside her. Now that fire fought to rage out of control. "Was incredible."

"The kiss?" he asked, swallowing before he teased, "Or the drive?" His near-gold gaze searched hers.

"All of it," she murmured. She wanted his touch and his kiss… And when his lips brushed softly against hers, she almost forgot there were still things to say. Important things… But his mouth was heaven. She shuddered, putting a hand in the middle of his chest.

"What's wrong?" His arms kept her anchored against him. Right where she wanted to be.

"Before I lose my head over you, you have to know this can't be more than what it is. Yes, you set me on fire—" She broke off, loving the smile on his face. "It doesn't change anything, though. I'm still leaving. And you're still juggling a dozen jobs and your girls. We both have kids to think about, and our fathers' determination to hate each other doesn't help. Neither of us is looking for more complications right now. But we're both lonely, both needing something the other can give."

He stared at her, his expression blank.

"I can't believe I'm saying this." She shook her head. "You're important to me, Brody. And now that we've reconnected, you're too important to lose over whatever this…is." She pointed back and forth between them. She'd never hurt him, ever. Or risk a friendship she'd always treasured. Right now, she needed his friendship. "I think it'd be easier if we kept this to ourselves. But this is kind of hard to get around, isn't it? The wanting? I just don't want us to do something we might regret." She ran a hand over her face. "Does that make me a bad person?"

His hands gripped the waist of her pants, the ghost of a smile on his lips. "Just so I understand what you're saying, here. You want me, I want you, and as long as we don't let it interfere with our friendship, or our families, we should see where this takes us?"

She smiled. "Yes. You made that sound easy."

His gaze searched hers, the muscle in his jaw working. "And you want to know if this makes you a bad person?"

She nodded, her smile vanishing.

"If you're a bad person, then so am I because I'm not

going to turn you down." His hand brushed the hair from her forehead. "Thought a lot about this?"

"All night." Which was true.

He nodded. "Sneaking around and keeping secrets? In Fort Kyle?" His hand cupped her cheek, one finger sweeping her lower lip. "Easier said than done."

His touch was too much. But his words struck a nerve. Maybe she was fooling herself. How could they get away with this? "Maybe."

"Maybe? Not so sure now?" he asked. "Might be too risky?" He leaned forward to run his nose along her throat. "I'm not trying to change your mind. I'm all for it, Goldilocks. But, like you said, neither one of us needs complications. So you let me know when you're sure this is what you really want to do." He released her and stepped away, leaving her reeling and flushed and oh-so needy. "I'm good with whatever you decide."

Whatever *she* decided. She wasn't sure why that bothered her. Almost like he'd be perfectly fine to forget last night happened. Yes, that would be easier. But she didn't know how to do that.

"I'll let you know about when we get the truck hauled in." He was talking about trucks and phone numbers, acting like nothing out of the normal was happening. Her body was one throbbing pulse, thanks to him. He was sliding on his coat, putting on his hat, getting ready to leave. And she just stood there, staring and beyond confused.

He opened the door but looked back at her. "You look beautiful today, India." And with that, he was gone.

What had just happened? She stared out the window. Disappointment slammed into her, hard and urgent. He was leaving. Acting like he was fine either way. *Which is good.* She was the one who had told him how it was going to be—then panicked when he pointed out it might not be as easy as they'd like. She'd regret it, if they got caught. But she knew, deep down, she'd regret not taking the risk more. If she were being honest, the risk made it only more exciting—something she hadn't had much of in years.

His headlights turned on, spurring her into action. She grabbed her phone to type, I'm sure. I think it will be worth the risk, but realized he had her number but she didn't have his. She headed to the door, but he was already driving down Main Street, his taillights disappearing in the rain.

BRODY TURNED OFF Main Street, his windshield wipers on high. Not that the rain could shake his good mood. India Boone was giving him a chance. She might not know it, thinking she could do this no-strings thing, but he'd do his damnedest to show her just how good it could be between them—and not just in bed. Sure, her proposal had thrown him for a loop. But he understood. She was still too hell-bent on getting away from this place to ever get involved with a man who called Fort Kyle home. It would take time, charm and sheer determination, but he'd show her the town was bigger and better than the bad blood between her and her father. And having her in his bed… His hands tightened on the steering wheel at the thought. He'd never wanted a woman as powerfully as he wanted India.

The rain picked up, forcing him to slow and turn his attention to driving. Fort Kyle needed water, but this had all the earmarks of a flash flood. Too much rain too quick led to washed-out fences, stranded livestock and accidents.

For years, he'd ached to hold India close, to have her

pressed against him, clinging to his shirt and kissing him as if her life depended on it. Last night she had. Nothing had felt better—felt more right—than that kiss.

Now she was offering him a whole lot more than just kisses. And while his heart was on the line, he'd risk it. She was worth it. To see her smile and laugh, to make her happy and love her the way he'd always wanted. For now, he had what he always wanted. Yep, he was feeling pretty damn lucky.

Lucky or not, he was feeling like an idiot when he pulled under the covered driveway of the feed store and parked. He had no doubt Jared, the man who ran Wallace Feed Store and Farm Equipment, was scratching his head over Brody's need to pick up supplies now—in the middle of the biggest storm these parts had seen for years. But if he hadn't come into town for *supplies*, he'd have had no excuse to see India. His cover story about the girls' birthday was a bit flimsy on its own.

"Jared." He nodded at the old man.

"Brody." The man nodded back. "Luke, give Mr. Wallace a hand, boy."

Brody shouldered a fifty-pound bag of feed and carried it to his truck. Jared's teenage nephew Luke helped him load his truck bed with five bags of feed, ten bags of deer corn, protein and salt blocks, a few rolls of barbed wire and a new post hole digger.

"Hell of a rain," Jared Beasley said, his battered feed store hat pushed back on his head. "Fence wash out?" he asked, eyeing the new wire.

"Not yet." Brody grinned. "But I want to be prepared in case."

"How's your father?" Jared had been working at the feed store for as long as Brody could remember. The man had well-creased leather skin and a piercing gaze, and he kept his ear to the ground. He was fair and honest—two things Vic Wallace valued above all else. Which made Jared one of his father's favorite employees.

"Stubborn as a mule and twice as mean," he answered, laughing with Jared.

"Sounds about right." The older man nodded, still grinning.

"But he's healing," Brody tacked on. "He's supposed to be taking it easy, but I don't see him listening for much longer." He pulled a tarp from his toolbox and shook it out, then tied it securely over his truck bed to keep his supplies dry.

"That's it, Mr. Wallace," Luke said, nodding at him. "Need anything else?"

"That should do it. Thank you, Luke."

The boy nodded, glanced out into the thick sheets of rain and headed back inside.

With a wave for Jared, Brody climbed into the truck. His phone started ringing. He sighed, pulled his phone out and answered it. His mother. When she learned he was in town, she rattled off a small grocery list, including food for Lollipop, who had a sensitive stomach.

He hung up and was about to pull out when his phone started ringing again, but this time it wasn't his mother.

"Brody Wallace? Jan Ramirez here. From WQAI, channel four. Edna Francis contacted me about your run for mayor." WQAI was one of the only local news stations—in the city of Alpine forty minutes down the road.

This was probably what Miss Francis had called him about. "Did she?" He chuckled. "That woman is full of surprises."

"Yes, sir. She's quite a fan." He could hear the smile in the woman's voice. "And she's convinced me that I need to interview you," she said.

He paused. "Oh? I know firsthand how persuasive she can be." She'd talked him into running for mayor, after all.

She laughed. "You're smart to have her on your campaign, Mr. Wallace. Her enthusiasm is contagious. We'd like to do a segment on you and your family. A sort of re-introduction to the community as Fort Kyle's next mayor. You know, a real human interest story."

He should be flattered—thrilled at the exposure—but he wasn't.

"Would you be free Saturday? We'll come down, spend the day with you, and then air segments all next week at the five and ten o'clock news." She paused, clearly waiting for his response.

He cleared his throat, processing. He might be running unopposed, but he'd be working with neighboring towns and counties—this would give them a look at who he was and what he stood for. For that, he was thankful.

"Mr. Wallace?"

"Might want to hold off until this rain clears. Hate to have ya'll washed into a ravine on my account."

She laughed. "According to our weatherman, the rain should clear out before eight tonight. Where would you like to meet?"

"The fort." It was neutral territory—the perfect place for determining just how up close and personal Jan Ramirez needed to get with the rest of his family.

"Perfect. We'll plan to be there around ten?"

"Sounds like a plan." A plan that could blow up in his face. "I look forward to meeting you in person." They exchanged a few more pleasantries before he hung up, hoping like hell he hadn't just shot himself in the foot.

He hurried through the grocery store and then checked

out, sighing at the astronomical price of the dog food his mother had special-ordered.

By the time he was headed back to the ranch, he was soaking wet. He'd be lucky to get home in time for dinner and playtime with the girls before bed. He grinned, thinking about how tickled Amberleigh would be over the dinosaur Band-Aids he'd found. They weren't dragons, but they were close.

He pulled into the barn and parked. His phone rang. "Brody here."

"Hey, Brody, it's Daniel. I'm taking the tow truck out to pick up the truck on the ridge. I'll tow it back to Click's place and take a look at it there. As soon as I know what we're looking at, I'll let you know."

"Thanks, Daniel, I appreciate it. If the roads are too bad, don't take any chances."

"Nah, man, I kick it into four-wheel drive and have some fun. See ya," he said, and hung up.

Brody pulled India's number from his pocket, texted her the news and stared at the screen. He had so much more to say. In person. He ran through the rain to the house—groceries in tow.

"Wipe your feet," his mother called out.

"It won't make a difference. Might as well bring me a towel," he argued, standing on the welcome mat.

"Daddy!" Suellen came barreling at him, coming to a complete halt a foot away. "You're wet, Daddy."

"I am, sugar. It's raining buckets out there," he agreed. "Can you get a towel from Nana?"

Suellen nodded and ran off.

"Daddy's making a mess," Marilyn chastised him.

"Think I'll get in trouble?" he asked.

Marilyn shrugged.

Amberleigh came running, her bare feet splashing in the puddle he'd made before reaching for him.

"I'm wet," he warned.

"'Kay," she said, undeterred.

He set the bags on the ground and scooped her up, his phone falling from his pocket in the process. It hit the floor, bounced into the puddle and landed faceup.

"Uh-oh," Marilyn said. "Broke it?" She picked it up and offered it to him.

The screen lit up, no sign of damage. "I think it's fine." He took it, touching the screen. And revealing a new message. From India.

Thanks for the update. And that other thing. I'm sure. It will be worth the risk.

"Okay?" Amberleigh asked, tugging on his hand.

It will be worth the risk.

His heart tripped faster, those six words confirming this was his lucky day. There was no denying it would be risky, but not the way she thought. She didn't know he was risking his heart for her. She didn't know how much he loved her. But, this was his chance to win her over. She'd come to see him as the man she needed, a man who would love and respect her, and who wanted to make her happy—in every way he could.

He hugged Amberleigh tight and pressed a kiss to her temple, all the while smiling from ear to ear. "Everything is just fine, darling."

Chapter Eight

India wiped the scraps of construction paper and dried drops of glue off the laminate tabletop and into the trash can. Cal, always eager to help, had already swept the floor and was reading through the classroom books.

"India, you don't have to do that." Norma Klein was the lead first-grade teacher at Fort Kyle Elementary. She was patient and kind and hugely pregnant.

"I don't mind," she assured her. John, one of two custodians for all three grade schools, was always running. If wiping down the tables and chairs helped even a little, India was glad to do it. "How are you holding up?" she asked, remembering how tired she'd been at the end of her pregnancy with Cal.

"Almost ready," she said, leaning against the doorway. "And that's sort of why I came to find you."

India finished putting the chairs on the table. "What can I do to help?"

"Sub for me?" she asked. "With the holidays factored in, I'll be out until the first of February—assuming she doesn't come early."

"Long term?" Long term meant more money—a good thing. But she wasn't ready to let go of the idea that she and Cal would be long gone by February. With her counseling test coming up next month, she'd hopefully have a job by the holidays. But then, staying would give her more time with Brody. His arms. His smile. His touch. His kiss. A shudder ran up her spine. And more money—that would be the primary reason she stayed. If she stayed.

"Please," Norma said. "You know my kids and our schedule. You know how hard it is to find qualified substitutes." Considering how isolated Fort Kyle was, the pickings were slim. "You don't have to decide right away," Norma said, sensing her hesitation. "I know you need to focus on your test and all."

"I'll let you know soon, Norma. Thank you for asking me." Having a guaranteed income would be a nice change. And, even if she did pass her certification test, there was no guarantee she'd find a position right away. Still, the idea of staying put was a hard pill to swallow. The tension between her and her father was growing unbearable.

"Otherwise, I'll call my aunt, Betty Berry." She wrinkled her nose.

India tried not to react. "I didn't know Mrs. Berry was your aunt." Betty Berry was a retired teacher with years of experience, who still subbed occasionally. She was also old, impatient and hard of hearing. Her teaching methods hadn't changed since the 1970s. And most of the kids were scared of her.

"Yep. She's my mother's sister." She chuckled. "No more fun during family holidays than in the classroom." Norma waved. "Have a good weekend."

"You, too."

"Mom," Cal spoke up as soon as Norma left. "Why won't you help Mrs. Klein? Scary Berry is mean, Mom, really mean."

"Scary Berry?" she asked, trying not to laugh.

"She's awful." He put his book on the shelf and helped her put the last of the chairs up. "She makes you eat all your veggies at lunch."

"I'll have to ask her what her secret is," she teased.

"Mom." Cal frowned. "You have to color in the lines or she'll take recess away."

India sighed. "How about we talk about this later? Right now I want some caffeine, a clean shirt and a movie. Maybe a superhero movie? Or something with dinosaurs?"

Cal smiled. "Distracting me, Mom?"

She laughed. "Maybe." She did need a clean shirt, though. A kindergartner's strawberry milk carton had exploded all over her at lunch, leaving a residual stickiness even after spot treating.

"Can we go to the fort tomorrow? Take my arrowhead to Miss Ada and see if it's important?"

"I'm sure it is, Cal." She smiled at her son. He was probably the only five-year-old who worried about turning in his archeological finds. "We'll go as soon as they open, okay?"

"Okay," he agreed. "Can we watch *Journey to the Center of the Earth*?"

"For the hundredth time?" she asked. "Fine. But we need to make a grocery trip first, okay?"

He sighed but nodded as they walked down the hall to the office, then waited patiently while she signed out.

"Mom," he whispered. "Isn't that Mrs. Wallace?"

India glanced at the front desk. "Yes, it is," she agreed, wondering why the older woman was here.

"Cal!" Amberleigh came running at her son, all smiles.

"Hey, Amberleigh." He grinned. "What are ya'll doing here?"

"School," Amberleigh said with a shrug. "Hi." The little girl smiled up at India.

"Hi, Amberleigh," she said, crouching. "You're coming to school here? Cal really likes it."

She nodded.

"Not yet, Amberleigh," Mrs. Wallace said, coming to stand by her granddaughter. "We're just checking."

"I want school like Cal," Marilyn said, tugging on Mrs. Wallace's skirt.

"I love school." Suellen spun, singing, "School. School. School."

"I do, too," India agreed.

"You have to do more than color," Cal said. "You have to make letters and words and numbers, too."

The girls stared at him, listening as he listed off all the things they'd do at school. India smiled at the older woman, unsure how to proceed. She had no desire to be embroiled in the drama between their families—but that didn't mean Mrs. Wallace would feel the same. The only way to find out was to try. "They seem very excited about starting school."

Mrs. Wallace studied her before answering. "They seem more excited about your son."

"He's a good boy," India said, answering honestly. "Likes to make friends."

"I noticed that, the other evening." Mrs. Wallace's gaze was curious. "My Brody was that way when he was little. Still is. Boy never met a stranger."

She remembered. Brody had been a lot like Cal as a boy. Empathetic. Smart. Patient. He was friends with everyone. She'd been so drawn to his open smile, and she still was. Not that she was going to talk about Brody with his mother. "They are precious," she said, nodding at the girls.

Mrs. Wallace smiled at her granddaughters. "They are. And they're wearing me out."

India laughed. "I can imagine. One was hard enough. Starting school soon?"

The older woman's voice dropped. "It's going to be a while. They have to be four. They're turning three." She sighed.

Poor girls. And poor Mrs. Wallace. "Have you checked on the Mother's Day Out program at the church? It's a couple of hours on Monday, Wednesday and Friday. It might be just the thing," she suggested. "There's also story time at the library on Tuesday and Thursday mornings and craft time once a month. And the fort has family hikes and crafts, too—they put out a monthly calendar. It's not exactly school, but it gives you a few options to wear them out a little bit."

Mrs. Wallace looked surprised. "I had no idea. It's been some time since I've had to entertain little ones. This will be a real help. Thank you, India."

"My pleasure." She hesitated. "The girls and Cal get along. We'll be at the fort tomorrow around ten thirty. You're welcome to join us. We could explore one of the trails, if you like?"

There was a spark of excitement on Mrs. Wallace's face. "Tomorrow? Around ten thirty? I'd hate to intrude."

"Not at all. I think Cal is enjoying the hero worship." She pointed at her son, all three girls gathered around him.

Mrs. Wallace chuckled. "If you're sure, I think we can make that. The girls have mentioned Cal a few times." She watched as Cal led the girls down the hall to the trophy case. The girls were paying close attention, hanging on his every word. "Is it just you and Cal?"

India nodded.

"Good you have family to help out. Like Brody. Family is important when you've got children to raise." Mrs. Wallace frowned, her voice rising. "Amberleigh, you have to keep your shoes on to go to school."

"She's right," Cal said, pointing at his feet. "In school, you have to wear shoes."

Amberleigh sighed but put her shoe back on.

Mrs. Wallace's brows rose before she smiled. "Well, now, that was something. She won't wear her shoes for anyone," she whispered to India. "Let's go, girls. Your daddy will want to hear all about your visit."

India smiled, imagining the girls excitedly sharing their day with Brody. And Brody, being Brody, would give them their full attention. It was plain to see he adored his girls—as it should be. Cal wandered back to them, the girls trailing behind, chattering among themselves.

"You going home, too?" Marilyn asked him. "To your daddy?"

"Just me and Mom," Cal said.

"Oh," Suellen said, looking confused.

India glanced at her son, hating the glimpse of longing on his face. If she had it her way, Cal would have a father who hung on his every word. A man who would see her son as the brilliant and sweet boy he was.

Cal shrugged. "We're gonna watch a dinosaur movie."

Marilyn and Suellen looked horrified, but not Amberleigh. She looked delighted. So delighted that India wished she could invite the little girls over to play dinosaurs with Cal. But how would that work? Mrs. Wallace seemed at ease with the children's developing friendship—but the likelihood of her father and Mr. Wallace taking it in stride was slim. Instead, she and Cal helped

Mrs. Wallace herd the girls back into their Suburban. Amberleigh asked Cal questions about dinosaurs until the car door was closed. Mrs. Wallace waved her good-byes and drove off.

"Mom," Cal said, watching the vehicle disappear. "Think I'll ever get a brother or sister?"

It was the last question she'd expected him to ask. "I thought you liked being just me and you."

"I do." He took her hand. "But it might be nice to have someone to play with, too. I wouldn't mind a little sister like Amberleigh. She likes the same things I do."

"Except shoes," she teased, trying to shake off the sharp sting of tears Cal's words stirred. Her son wasn't the only one missing something. There was a time when all she'd wanted was a big family and a loving husband. But her husband had been anything but loving. And she couldn't have risked bringing another child into the world—not if JT was the father.

"She put them on for me," Cal said, grinning up at her. "I think I'd be a good big brother."

"I know you would, Cal," she agreed. "But I can't pick up a little brother or sister at the grocery store so—"

"I know that, Mom." He rolled his eyes. "You have to get married. Aunt Scarlett told me. We just need to find a man we both like."

She laughed then. "Is that all?"

"Seems simple enough," he said, climbing into the ranch work truck and buckling his seat belt. "You're pretty and nice and I'm a good kid. We'll find someone, get married, and I can be a big brother."

India closed the door, scrambling for an appropriate response for her son. How could she explain that, right now, the only man she was interested in was the one she couldn't marry?

BRODY NODDED AT the aging structures that made up Fort Kyle. "This place has seen a lot of history. I'd like it to be around for future generations."

Jan Ramirez, the channel four reporter, nodded. "So historical preservation is important to you?"

"Yes." He paused, his gaze drifting over the newly green vegetation. Amazing how quickly the rains had perked up the West Texas landscape. Flowers blossomed overnight, scenting the fresh air and adding bold strokes of color. There was no denying it was rugged country. But it was home. "It's more than the fort. It's our way of life. Places like Fort Kyle are hard to find. We know our neighbors, and we take care of each other. Working hard and taking pride in what we do—in our town—is a way of life. Families vacation here for that reason, I think. Sure, there's plenty to do. Outdoors and festivals and such. But it's also the heritage, and the sense that—since internet connections and cell service is patchy at best out here—you can still escape to a simpler time."

Jan's expression shifted, her smile softening. "Some people would say that not being connected is a drawback."

"It's a choice, isn't it?" He chuckled, shaking his head. "I guess it depends on how you look at it. I'd like to think that our community is more connected and present because they're not plugged in all the time."

"So you're glad you moved back home?" She had an easy conversational style that almost made him forget the cameraman following them around the fort.

"I am. I'm glad my girls will grow up here." He nodded. "And I'm glad to do what I can to keep Fort Kyle a place people love to call home and love to visit again and again."

Jan nodded. "I think that's good for now, Marco. We'll do some more at lunch." She spoke to the cameraman.

"I'll check feed," he said, heading back to the WQAI van.

Jan inspected the fort, her gaze traveling over the red brick structures built with their backs against the sheer face of the equally red cliffs. As defense went, it was smart—preventing any chance of rear attack. A long flagpole stood in the middle of the yard, the American and Texas flags blowing in the breeze. "I've never been here before."

Brody nodded. "It's quite a place."

"Miss Francis was right, Brody, I'm impressed," she said. "Not many men would give up the wealth and connections you'd made for yourself in the big city only to come home and take care of your parents and the family businesses."

"That makes it all sound so selfless." He grinned. "Truth was, I was already done. It took some time for me to realize I'm not big-city material. This place made me who I am. I want my girls to grow up like that, in a place where people care about them. Where things, maybe, aren't so confusing." His gaze wandered around the property, lingering on the barracks he and his Scout troop had painted for a badge. He grinned. "Speaking of my girls." He nodded at his mother's Suburban, pulling into the lot next to the information center.

"I can't wait to meet them. Triplets. That's a full-time job right there." Jan turned, shielding her eyes in the morning sun. "Your girlfriend?" she asked.

He chuckled. "My mother."

She glanced his way, then back at the Suburban.

He headed toward the Suburban, the squeals and calls of "Daddy" greeting him long before he'd reached the car. He was smiling like a fool by the time Suellen came barreling his way. He hugged her against his legs. Then Marilyn. "Having a good morning?" he asked.

"Yep," Suellen said.

"Yes, Daddy," Marilyn said, tugging on his jeans. "Not Amberleigh."

"No?" he asked. Amberleigh had yet to emerge from the Suburban. "Shoes giving her problems?"

"Boots," Suellen offered.

"Let's go see if we can help." He took a small hand in each of his and headed back to the Suburban.

"No," Amberleigh said, holding her foot up as high as her car seat would allow.

"Amberleigh." His mother's tone was cajoling. "You can't go stomping around here without boots on. There are cactuses. And scorpions. And sharp rocks." She paused. "Cal will be here soon. He'll be wearing boots."

Amberleigh stopped flailing around then. "Cal?"

"Cal's coming?" Brody asked, surprised on many levels.

"They didn't tell you?" his mother asked. "He was at the school yesterday, with his mother. The four of them got on, so his mother told us they were coming out here this morning—if we wanted to join them."

India was coming. Here? Now? The rain had left him buried in repairs and damage control, taking all his time and energy. He hadn't responded to her text because he wanted whatever happened next to happen face-to-face. But he'd never considered a scenario where his children *and* his mother were present.

Amberleigh was holding her boot, her big eyes staring out the Suburban door.

"Then I bet they'll be here soon," Brody said, hoping to encourage his daughter. "Better get ready."

Amberleigh sighed but put on her boot and climbed out of her seat—at the same time a white Fire Gorge truck pulled into the parking lot. "Cal?" Amberleigh asked, tugging on Brody's pants.

"It is," he agreed, his heart rate picking up enough to warn him to keep it together. Knowing that India wanted him was enough to make him happy—for now.

Two minutes later Cal was showing his daughters the arrowhead he'd found close to his cabin.

"Pokey?" Marilyn asked.

"A little," he said. "You can touch it."

Suellen and Marilyn shook their heads and stepped back. Amberleigh leaned close, running a single finger along the smooth flint stone in the boy's hand.

"That's a good one," Brody said, doing his best not to get distracted by India. She'd slowly made her way out of the Fire Gorge truck to stand, ten feet away, lingering by the hood.

"What did you find?" Jan Ramirez asked, joining them—her cameraman in tow.

"An arrowhead," Cal said, not bothering to look up. "It's for Miss Ada to keep here at the fort."

"That's nice of you." Jan smiled. "Are you going to be an archeologist when you grow up?"

He looked up then. "Paleontologist, probably."

"Pal-e-o-what?" Suellen asked.

"Someone who studies dinosaurs," Brody said. "Cal is all about the dinosaurs."

"Cal," India called. "Let's go give it to Ada. Come on, Tanner."

Tanner jumped out of the open window of the truck and trotted up the path, following Cal.

"You getting this?" Jan Ramirez asked, smiling back at the cameraman.

Brody glanced at India, noting the concern on her face and the stiffening of her posture. He waved, but she was too preoccupied with the camera to notice. She hurried Cal into the information center, had Tanner sit on the porch and closed the door behind them.

What was that about?

"You don't need me anymore, do you?" his mother asked. "I'll go back and get your daddy's lunch in the oven."

"Thanks," he said, handing over his truck keys and taking the keys to the Suburban in exchange. "We'll be out in a few hours. You need me to bring anything home?"

His mother glanced at the camera, turned a bright shade of pink, shook her head and hurried to his truck.

"These are your girls?" Jan asked.

"Suellen. Marilyn. And Amberleigh." Amberleigh was tugging his hand with all her might, leaning all her weight toward the information center.

"It's nice to meet you," Jan said. "I'm Jan and this is Marco. Marco has lots of kids, too. Six?" she asked.

"Seven," he said.

"Wow." Brody shook his head. "You've got my respect."

Marco chuckled at the same time Suellen asked, "What's that?" She pointed at the large camera on Marco's shoulder.

"It's a camera," Jan said. "Do you girls ever watch movies?"

All three of them nodded.

"We're making a movie about your daddy," she said. "You want to be in it?"

Suellen and Marilyn nodded, but Amberleigh hid behind his legs. He bent and scooped her up, her little arms twining around his neck as she buried her face against his shoulder. "Feeling shy, sugar?" he whispered.

Amberleigh nodded.

"That's okay." He lifted her into his arms and patted her back.

"We can get some wide shots of the kids running around the fort," Marco suggested. "Give them some time to warm up to the camera?"

Marco headed out to find the optimal spot to film, leaving him with the girls and Jan. He kept glancing at the information center, but there was no sign of Cal or India. Was she hiding from him? Or the camera?

"Want Cal," Amberleigh whispered.

"You do?" Brody asked.

"Who is Cal?" Jan asked. "A cousin?" She eyed the truck, the Fire Gorge logo hard to miss. "Someone who works for the Boones?"

"Friend," Marilyn said. "Likes dino—dinoroars."

Jan smiled. "Right, the paleontologist."

"He and Amberleigh both like dinosaurs. And dragons," Brody explained.

"His mother is awfully familiar. I've seen her before." Jan glanced at the information center.

"Probably. That's India Boone." Brody did his best to keep his tone neutral.

"Boone?" The excitement in the woman's eyes set off warning bells. "As in Woodrow Boone? Is she one of his daughters? You're friends with a Boone? What about the Wallace-Boone feud?"

Brody shook his head. "No feud here. The Boones are an important family in these parts. They are my neighbors. The feud is between the patriarchs, not the families."

Jan Ramirez nodded. "Miss Francis said you were a dreamer."

Brody chuckled, shifting Amberleigh to his other arm. "I guess I am, Miss Ramirez. But a person should have dreams. It gives life adventure and purpose."

"Daddy. Get Cal?" Amberleigh asked. "Please."

"We'll check in with him later, okay? Let's go explore the fort." He smiled at his daughter.

Her reaction was a complete surprise. Amberleigh's face turned bright red, she opened her mouth and let out the most bloodcurdling scream he'd ever heard. And she kicked off her boots—sending one into a clump of flowers and the other smack-dab into Jan Ramirez's forehead.

Chapter Nine

India and Cal were listening to Ada's take on the origins of Cal's arrowhead when a horrible shriek pierced the air. Tanner started barking, on instant alert.

"Oh goodness, did someone get hurt?" Ada asked, hurrying toward the back. "Better get the first aid kit."

"Come on, Mom," Cal called before dashing out the door, Tanner on his heels.

India followed, the little girl's cry too intense to ignore. She ran down the rocky path, her heart pounding. Poor sweet Amberleigh was gasping and wailing in her daddy's arms. Marilyn and Suellen each held on to one of Brody's legs, but neither of them was crying—yet.

Tanner circled, whimpering and barking. "Heel, Tanner." Cal placed a hand on the dog's head before asking Amberleigh, "Get stung?"

"Nope." Brody was frowning.

"A cactus needle?" India asked, knowing how much the little girl hated shoes. She'd been wearing boots. Now she was barefoot. Why would Brody let her take her shoes off here? One glance at Brody told her he hadn't.

"Nope." Brody shook his head, studying his daughter. He wasn't happy.

"You hurt, sweetie?" Ada asked, clutching the first aid kit to her chest.

Brody shook his head. "She's fine, Miss Ada. I'm sorry she got you all worked up."

"Well, what's the matter, Amberleigh?" Cal asked, sensing something was off. "You're screaming so loud you'll scare off the horny toads and grasshoppers I was gonna show you."

Amberleigh drew in a shuddering breath and was instantly quiet. She stared at Cal with huge light brown eyes and nodded. "O-okay," she whispered.

Brody's frown grew. "Amberleigh May Wallace. Did you just throw a fit to get Cal's attention?"

Amberleigh stared up at her father with big eyes. Her lower lip flipped down, quivering fiercely, as she nodded. In that instant, India was smitten. Poor, sweet little thing wasn't good with her words. She'd wanted Cal, and Cal wasn't coming. What else could she do? The little girl felt bad about it, that much was obvious.

Cal sighed, staring up at Amberleigh and putting both hands on his hips. "I was coming. I just had to give Miss Ada my arrowhead."

"'Kay," Amberleigh whispered again. "S-sorry," she hiccupped.

India patted Amberleigh's back, wanting to calm her. "It's okay, sweetie. We were worried about you, that's all. We're happy you're okay."

"I'm glad *she's* okay." The television reporter was rubbing her forehead. "Who knew something so little could pack such a punch?" She was smiling, but there was an undeniable edge to her voice.

"I'm so sorry, Jan. She didn't mean to hit you in the head with her boot." Brody was upset by his daughter's outburst and, possibly, a bit amused. "She's really sorry. Aren't you, Amberleigh? Everything is fine, girls."

Suellen and Marilyn let go of him, but stayed close.

Amberleigh nodded, her lower lip trembling again and her big eyes filling with tears.

India couldn't stop herself from looking at the red bump popping up on Jan Ramirez's forehead. Not the best look for a news reporter. And yet, it *was* an accident. Amberleigh might have thrown a fit, but she'd never meant to hurt someone.

"It's okay, sweetie. Accidents happen," India said, still patting the little girl's back.

And just like that, Amberleigh was leaning away from her father and toward her, arms and fingers stretching. "May I?" she asked.

Brody sighed, relinquishing his daughter to her. "Sure."

The little girl's slight weight in her arms was heaven. Her little head rested on India's shoulder while her little hand slid through India's hair. "You're all right now," India said, keeping her tone as soothing as possible. "Your daddy loves you, Cal is here and we'll go find some horny toads."

Tanner barked, looking back and forth between Cal and Amberleigh.

"She's okay, Tanner," Cal told the dog. The dog's ears drooped and he trotted off to explore.

"Horn-toads?" Amberleigh asked.

"Sorta like baby dinosaurs. Or dragons. Spiky backs and fast runners. But they don't have wings and they don't breathe fire."

Amberleigh perked up, smiling at her, then Cal. The other two weren't quite so enthusiastic, but they didn't protest, either.

India shook her head, her gaze colliding with Brody's. Collided and stuck, the force of magnetism cementing the hold and stoking the fire in her belly. She welcomed the burn.

How could he do this to her? With just one look?

It was just Brody. The same Brody who had bought her circus peanuts when her guinea pig had died in second grade. The same Brody who helped her break into the girl's high school locker room to get her purse—and avoid another argument with her father. The same Brody who made her believe she could do whatever she set her mind to. So when had looking at him made her feel like *this*? Warm and flushed and light-headed and...beautiful.

Brody stared right back at her. There was no misinterpreting the look in his tawny eyes. She wasn't the only one strapped into this odd, wonderful emotion-charged roller coaster. His attention was very clearly focused on her. And her mouth. Which was bad, considering Ada Haynes and a newscaster were both watching the exchange with open curiosity.

He shouldn't look at her that way. He shouldn't make her feel this way. They were going to have to seriously work on the *secret* part of this arrangement.

She patted Amberleigh on the back and stepped away from Brody, needing space between them. "Cal, stick to the fort path." It was long enough to wear them out and short enough to not require anyone to be carried back. It was also well traveled, keeping the wildlife less likely to surprise them on their trek.

"Yes, ma'am," Cal said, excited. "More lizards that way. Come on, Tanner."

"Let Tanner go first," she said, watching the dog trot ahead, almost as if he understood what she needed from him. There were times she thought the dog really did understand her, especially when it came to keeping Cal safe.

"The lizards will be hunting bugs." Cal was already

intently scouring the landscape for signs of the palm-sized horned lizards native to the area.

"Bugs?" Suellen asked. "I have a worm."

"Worms are cool," Cal said, earning a smile from Suellen.

She followed, determined to hide whatever craziness was happening between her and Brody.

It was a pretty day, the sort of day meant for enjoying. All she was going to think about was the beautiful baby on her hip and her adorable son playing tour guide for two more equally precious girls.

"Here." Brody's hand circled her upper arm, gently stopping her. He made a show of checking inside Amberleigh's boots before sliding them back onto his daughter's feet. "She can walk now."

His hand stayed where it was, holding her close, his scent teasing her, making her every nerve sit up and take notice of him. It was torture—and he knew it. His eyes were sparkling as she pulled away, gently, and sucked clear air deep into her lungs. "I don't mind," India said, continuing to pat Amberleigh's back. "Besides, shouldn't you be mayor-ing it up?" she said, glancing over his shoulder at the WQAI van. "She came all this way for you."

"In heels. She said something about an ice pack in the van." His grin made her laugh. "You have a pretty laugh, India Boone. Doesn't she, Amberleigh?"

Amberleigh smiled. "Pretty."

"She is that," he agreed. "India's got a big heart, too, Amberleigh. In here." He tapped his daughter's chest. "Nothing better on this earth than a big heart."

Amberleigh nodded, as if she was in full agreement.

His compliments lit her up on the inside. And set off warning bells. So she downplayed his praise. "I don't have a camera, Brody. You don't have to turn on the charm with me."

"Maybe you're the one I want to charm." He studied her closely, smiling at the heat that stung her cheeks.

It was too much. He was too much. And she liked it.

He was smiling at her when he said, "Your truck is at Click's place. Hope to have it fixed in a few days."

"That's great news, Brody, thank you." And it was. Now all she had to do was figure out how to pay for the repairs. Between the test fees, upcoming holidays and her truck repairs, maybe she *should* take the long-term substitute job.

He smiled at her, and that smile, oh that smile. It was hard to think about practicality when faced with something so damn beautiful.

She wasn't going to stare at him. Or get caught up in his eyes. Nope, she focused on Cal and the girls. "Be careful picking up rocks, Cal."

"Yes, ma'am," he called back, pointing at something in the leaves. Tanner was rigid, ears and tail standing up straight and alert.

"What is it?" she called. "Tanner?"

Tanner's stance never changed.

Cal called back. "Just an armadillo."

Brody ran past her. "Stay there. Don't move."

"You hear him, Cal? Stay put." India followed quickly, shifting Amberleigh to her other side out of instinct.

"It's okay. It's not close. Tanner won't let it get anywhere near us," Cal said. "It's hiding in those leaves over there."

Brody stepped in front of the kids, his gaze pinpointing the spot Cal indicated. "You've got good eyes, Cal." His posture relaxed. "Good boy, Tanner."

Tanner whimpered, his tail wagging. But the armadillo's presence made it impossible for him to be completely at ease. Protecting Cal was all that mattered to that dog. He wouldn't leave her son's side until the creature was gone.

Brody's voice was stern. "That's an armadillo. That's what's been tearing up Nana's garden."

India watched the little creature digging in the wet soil. They were a pest but weren't a real threat to people. They could carry all sorts of germs, though, so keeping the kids away was necessary.

"Is it bad?" Marilyn asked.

"It's not good," Cal said.

"They're just pesky, for the most part. But, to be safe, don't touch 'em," Brody said. "It can bite or scratch you and make you real sick."

Suellen backed up. "Bite us?"

Tanner tried to round the kids together, eager to herd them all to safety. "It's okay, Tanner," India whispered, rubbing the dog behind the ear.

"They look funny when they run," Cal said, pointing at the ridiculously tiny feet sticking out from under the armadillo's armor. "Bet there's lots of lizards up ahead. Come on, Amberleigh."

Amberleigh let go of India, so India put her down and watched the little girl run to catch up to Cal.

"Try to keep them together, Tanner," she said, nodding after the kids. The dog milled among them, doing his best to keep them in line while staying on alert.

"Good dog," Brody said, admiring the animal's efficiency.

"He was a stray," she said. "I almost hit him with my car when he was a puppy, all bony, floppy ears and big paws. JT told me to leave him, but I couldn't. He had the sweetest eyes and was so eager to love someone. I brought him home and cleaned him up—he was my baby until Cal came along. Then Tanner decided Cal was his baby, too. He takes good care of him."

Brody studied her for a long time. She knew what that look meant: he had questions. But he must have sensed her reticence because he didn't push. "My mom said Amberleigh put her shoes on because of Cal," Brody said, returning Suellen's wave.

India watched the exchange. There was no denying the love and devotion this man had for his daughters. And it made her ache. He was a good man. A good father. And Brody Wallace was, without a doubt, the best-looking man she'd laid eyes on in…years.

He turned when the news reporter came power-walking up the path.

"My running shoes were in the van," she explained. "I'm Jan Ramirez, WQAI. You're India Boone?"

"I am." She glanced nervously at Cal.

"How's the head?" Brody asked.

"It's fine." The woman waved his question aside. "You two are friends?"

India cleared her throat. "Just to be clear, my son and I aren't interested in being part of this interview."

Jan's gaze darted between the two of them. "You and Brody being friends will only confirm what a great guy he is."

India didn't take the bait. She wasn't going to talk about the feud or their fathers. "I'm sure you'll be able to do that without having me or my son on camera." She did her best to smile but knew it fell flat.

"May I ask why you don't want to be on film?" Jan pushed, her eyes narrowing slightly. "Are the two of you trying to keep your relationship a secret?"

India stopped, her heart in her throat. *Relationship?*

The word struck a nerve, a highly agitated nerve far too close to the surface. And the look on Jan Ramirez's face told her the other woman knew it, too.

Tanner's sudden barking distracted her. His barking sharpened, turning ferocious—and India's blood to ice. She didn't know what was happening, but the chorus of cries from Cal and the girls had her running toward them with her heart lodged in her throat.

BRODY HELD HIS BREATH, the terror and screams of his daughters setting him in motion.

"Snake! Snake!" Cal cried out. "Tanner! No!"

And there was Tanner, stumbling, then falling, to the ground, still whimpering.

Brody had never moved so fast in his life. He didn't think as he kicked aside the copperhead, which landed a few feet away and went slithering off. He didn't think as he herded the kids toward India, and bent to scoop up Tanner. "Cal. We need to get him to the clinic. Quick. Run back," Brody said, handing the boy his keys. "I'll get Tanner, you get the truck door?"

Cal nodded, gripping the keys and running as fast as his legs could carry him.

India was already picking up a wailing Suellen and Amberleigh, while Jan Ramirez awkwardly carried Marilyn.

How they managed to get back to the truck without further incident was a mystery. While India buckled the kids into the Suburban, Brody loaded Tanner into the back.

"I'll stay with him," India said, climbing into the back with the dog. "You did good, Tanner. You did good, baby." Tanner lay with his head in her lap while she rubbed her hand along his black-and-brown fur, crooning softly to him.

Brody's heart hurt, the tears on her cheeks gutting him. "It's going to be okay," he promised, closing the doors. He drove to town in a blur.

The arrival at the vet clinic, his mom arriving to take the girls to the Soda Shop, India going back with Tanner… Now, nothing. Waiting in an empty room.

"Is Tanner gonna be okay?" Cal asked, his legs swinging.

There were times Cal seemed so much older than he was. But now, sitting next to the boy, it was impossible to miss how small and young and scared he was. Brody wanted to comfort him, to tell him that his dog would be fine, but he knew giving the boy false hope would only hurt more. "I don't know, Cal," Brody answered honestly. "He's a big dog. That'll work in his favor." As far as he knew, snakebites were rarely fatal if they were treated early. Still, that damn snake bit Tanner right on the eye.

"He's tough," Cal said, his hands clasped in his lap.

Brody nodded, draping an arm around the boy's shoulders. "He is."

Cal looked up at him then, his big green-blue eyes so like his mother's. "He was protecting me." Those eyes flooded with tears.

"Of course he was," Brody agreed, patting Cal on the back. "You're his boy."

Cal nodded, sniffing loudly.

Brody squeezed Cal's shoulder. If Cal wanted to cry, he should cry. If he needed to be brave, Brody would sit quietly at his side. Whatever the boy needed. But, dammit, he felt like he should *do* something—say something. Just what that was, he had no idea. When India stepped out of the examination room, he could breathe a little easier.

"Cal," she said, squatting, her arms outstretched. "He's sleepy, but he's okay."

"Momma." Cal barreled into her arms. "Tanner's not gonna die, is he?"

"No, baby," she soothed. "He is not going to die." She hugged him close, burying her face against the side of his head and closing her eyes. She held him that way, a deep furrow forming between her brows, as they hugged. Sitting there, watching Cal and India cling to each other, was hard. He had room in his arms for both of them. Room in his heart, too.

Her eyes stayed closed but she said, "Thank you for keeping Cal company, Brody. Truly."

"Anytime," he murmured, his voice thick.

"Can I see him?" Cal asked. "Is that okay?"

"You can." She eased her hold on him and stood. "He's real sleepy from the medicine and he needs to stay still and quiet, okay?"

"Yes, ma'am. Coming, Brody?" he asked.

He glanced at India, not wanting to overstep. Her nod was all the encouragement he needed.

"Yes, sir," he said, earning a smile from India. Damn but he loved her, more than she'd ever know.

"Hey, Cal." The veterinary tech was India's cousin, Tandy Boone. She greeted them with a sympathetic smile. "You've got yourself one good dog, you know that?"

"He's a hero. Mom said he'll be okay?" Cal wanted reassurance.

"Yep. That tube gives him medicine and water—stuff to help him get better. It was good you got him here so fast." She hugged him. "I can't make any promises about his eye, Cal. We'll keep it covered and hope for the best, okay? But the rest of him will be just fine after a nice long rest." Tandy led them through the door at the back of the exam room. Brody stared around at what resembled a large surgery center with cages on each side. It was dated and old, but clean and orderly.

Tandy pointed. "There he is."

Tanner lay on a massive dog bed, his cage door propped open. Brody thought the dog was asleep until Tanner's long tail thumped in greeting.

"Hey, boy. Thank you. You're the best dog in the whole world," Cal whispered, dropping to his knees. "I love you, boy. You stay real still, okay?" he pleaded, placing his small hand on Tanner's side. "Me and Mom will take real good care of you." It was a promise.

India sat on the floor by Cal, one hand on her son, the other on the dog. Brody swallowed back the lump in his throat. Tanner was family. The three of them relied on each other—loved each other. And today had shaken that.

"He needs to stay with me tonight," Tandy said. "Just so we can keep an eye on him. Okay?"

"As long as he's gonna be fine. I don't care if his eye is broken," Cal said, his voice pinched and tight. "But he can come home tomorrow, though?"

"Yes, sir." Tandy stooped, looking the boy squarely in the eye. "Let's shake on it? So you'll feel better." She shook his hand. "When you come to get him tomorrow, I'll tell you what we need to do to take care of Tanner and get him back on his paws again, okay?" she said.

Cal nodded and wiped the back of his hand across his eyes. "Okay."

Brody hurt for the boy. And India. They'd had more than their fair share of loss and grief. Losing Tanner wasn't an option. Just like standing by, doing nothing, wasn't an option for him. He slowly made his way to where Tandy was making notes and whispered, "Can I do anything?"

Tandy shook her head. "He's had the antivenin and some antibiotics. Other than the topical ointment, there's not much to be done." She shrugged. "There's no guarantee he'll keep his eye, but he'll adapt easily."

One eye or two, Cal wouldn't care as long as he had his dog. But he remembered something India had said, something about paying for the truck repairs. "I'll take care of the bill," he whispered.

Tandy's brows rose. "Are you sure she'll be okay with that?"

He frowned. "No. She'll fight me tooth and nail." She was too determined to be independent—even when she could use the help. "Maybe you could help with that?" He paused. "You know, chalk it up to a family discount? Since she's your cousin? Something?"

Tandy glanced at India and Cal.

"I'd owe you."

She nodded slowly. "I'll figure something out. But you don't owe me a thing."

"I don't want to get you in trouble," he argued.

She rolled her eyes. "With who? I'm pretty much my own boss at this point. I'll be taking over the practice next year." She smiled. "Click told me, Brody. I know why you're doing this. Maybe it's time you told India how you feel?"

He stared at the woman, reeling. He'd never told a soul about his feelings for India Boone. So how the hell did Click Hale know? "I don't know what you're—"

"It's the way you look at her when you think no one's watching you. I've seen it myself, so don't try to tell me otherwise. I see it now." She patted his hand. "Click said it's always been that way."

Brody shook his head, his gaze shifting to India and Cal. He had more than most folks—he knew that. But, seeing them, he couldn't help but want more. He'd always loved her. He always would. And Cal? He was a good boy—a son a man could be proud of. "I'd appreciate it if you didn't share your observations with anyone."

She nodded. "Don't wait too long, Brody. I know India pretty well. She keeps her head down, planning what's next and how to get there. You need to get her to look up and see what's right here, in front of her. You, your girls and the family she's always wanted."

"Is that all?" he tried to tease, Tandy's words all too tempting.

She shrugged. "Or you let her go and you move on."

His stomach tightened. He'd let her go before, he could do it again—if it made her happy. But he'd never moved on.

"He's sleeping, Cal. We should let him get some rest," India said, pushing off the floor. "Tandy will call us if she needs us, okay?"

Cal pressed a kiss to the top of Tanner's head and stood, staring down at the dog. "I'll see you tomorrow, Tanner," he whispered.

"He'll be feeling better tomorrow, Cal. And, when he is, we'll come get him." India nodded, looking worn out. "You ready?"

They were a solemn, quiet group as they made their way back into the reception area. Cal did his best to put on a brave face, but by the time they left the clinic he was fighting back tears. One look at India told Brody she wasn't in much better shape.

"The girls are with their grandmother at the Soda Shop," Brody offered. "How about some lunch and ice cream?"

"How about some French fries and a root beer float? Sound good to you, Cal?" India asked with as much cheer as she could muster. It made Brody's heart hurt.

"A little." He paused. "He'll miss us, Mom."

India took Cal's hand in hers. "He will, but he'll be mostly sleeping. Like when you get sick? It helps him heal."

Cal nodded. "Okay."

"Tomorrow will be here before you know it," Brody tacked on.

Cal was quiet as they walked down the street, then asked, "Think Tanner'll be feeling well enough to ride with me in the cattle drive? If Papa lets me ride?"

India looked lost and more than a little defeated. "I don't know, Cal."

Cal nodded, his sniff echoing.

"You're going to ride?" Brody led them across the street, hoping the change in topic would rouse the boy's spirits. "Good for you. I started about your age, if I remember right."

Cal shrugged. "I'm not a real good rider yet. Papa's always real busy so…"

Brody watched the tightening of India's jaw. He'd gone and stuck his foot in it again. But, maybe, he could do something about it this time. "I can show you."

India came to a dead stop. "You don't have time for that, Brody. The girls, your family businesses, the campaign—it's *not* a good idea."

"Why not?" he and Cal asked in unison.

He couldn't stop the smile that spread across his face. And, finally, Cal was smiling a little, too.

"You *know* why not," India pleaded, her gaze searching his.

It would be so damn easy to pull her close and tell her

all the reasons why it was a very good idea. He'd do just about anything to chase the defeat from her eyes. And holding her close and comforting her sounded like the perfect place to start.

She seemed unwilling to share the weight of the world she shouldered—even if the weight might be crushing her. And he didn't understand it. Did he want to hold her and kiss her and tell her he loved her? Yes, but, he knew—to her—they were just friends. And friends helped each other out.

"Click has a bunch of horses. Your truck is at Click's. I'm Click's neighbor." He shrugged, holding open the door of the Soda Shop. "I'm happy to help. Your boy should know how to ride. He's a cowboy after all—from a founding family hereabouts."

"Then I could surprise Papa," Cal said. "He'd be proud to see me on a horse."

"I know he's already proud of you," Brody assured him. "You've got the makings of a fine young man. Someone I'm proud to call my friend." Cal lit up like a Christmas tree, trotting into the Soda Shop and heading straight for the girls to update them on Tanner's status.

"Brody." India's hand gripped his, stopping him. "I know you mean well, but..." She shook her head, searching for the right words. "He's had a lot of people disappoint him." India studied him, warning him away like a mother bear protecting her cub.

There was steel in her voice, a certain stiffness in her posture that earned his respect. And made him long to show her how good things could be. He wasn't her father. He wasn't Cal's father. He knew what it meant to love unconditionally. That was how he loved her—how he'd love Cal, if she gave him the chance.

He squeezed her hand, cradling it against his chest. "I promise you, I won't be one of them."

Chapter Ten

India felt the beat of Brody's heart against her hand. It was fast. No, not fast. Thundering. The concern in those tawny eyes reached down inside and melted the ice around her heart. No. Dammit. No. She had to fight this. Fight him.

"India?" he asked, tugging her aside of the door.

"Stop, please," she whispered. "You keep looking at me like that…"

He grinned, one brow cocking up. "Like I want you, India. I do. To be here for you."

Her breath escaped on a shudder. The memory of his hands gripping her against him, his lips sealed against hers, flashed through her eyes.

His eyes narrowed. "You want me to kiss you." He swallowed. "I'm happy to do it. Right here on Main Street in front of the whole damn town—"

"Stop." She covered his lips with her hand, startled when he pressed a kiss to her fingertips. The touch was a jolt to the system—racing down her arm, into her chest and low in her belly. It was heaven. The heat in his eyes was all that mattered.

No, it wasn't. They were out in the open, for crying out loud. Her gaze darted around what appeared to be an empty street. But half a dozen storefront windows lined the opposite side of the street. For all she knew, twice as many eyes were watching them—taking notes and making phone calls. And still, the feel of his lips kept her captive. What was she thinking? What was he thinking?

His eyes blazed with raw hunger, a hunger she shared.

"Behave," she whispered, tugging her hand from his and hurrying into the Soda Shop.

Cal sat with Brody's girls, talking animatedly. Ramona Wallace listened as well, looking a little shell-shocked and in need of reinforcements. Small puddles of ice cream covered the tabletop—along with a mountain of napkins and wet wipes.

"He's wearing a pirate patch over his bad eye, but he'll be okay," Cal finished.

She gripped the chair back, doing her best to steady her heart and her breathing. Even now, the look in Brody's eyes had her weak-kneed.

The girls clapped and laughed.

"I'm so glad," Mrs. Wallace said. "Suellen said he was quite the hero, knocking you out of the way before the snake struck."

Cal puffed up with pride. "He was a hero."

"You're lucky to have him." Mrs. Wallace smiled.

"We all were." Brody's voice made India jump, clinging to the chair back. "I told India and Cal to have some ice cream with us. Maybe some real food, too." He took a seat between his girls, his gaze finding hers.

"Mom wants French fries," Cal said. "Come on, Mom, sit down."

"Why bite Tanner?" Amberleigh asked.

"Snakes don't have arms or legs or hands or feet so I guess they have to do something to protect themselves," Cal said.

"I don't think I've ever heard it explained that way, Cal," Brody said. "But I'd say that's about right."

India wavered. She wasn't the least bit hungry for food. What she was craving sat four feet away, grinning like a fool—knowing damn well she was struggling.

It was the most awkward meal she'd ever shared. Poor Mrs. Wallace did her best to keep a conversation going, but India was too distracted by Brody. Brody, who seemed perfectly at ease. He laughed and talked with the kids, munched his cheeseburger and listened to all of Cal's dinosaur facts without batting an eye.

By the time she'd finished half of her French fries, the yearning of her body had spread. With every laugh and smile, every bad joke and eye roll, Brody Wallace made her yearn. Badly.

"Are you okay, India?" Mrs. Wallace asked, her voice low.

India nodded. Except she wasn't. Not in the least. "I think… I just need a minute? It's been a…day." She pushed back her chair and hurried into the bathroom.

The burn of tears took her by surprise. She stared at her reflection in the mirror, frowned at the red-rimmed, wide-eyed woman staring back and hurried into one of the stalls before her sobs found her.

There was no reason to cry.

Cal was safe. As long as she had Cal, everything was fine.

The girls—curious Marilyn, sweet Suellen and fearless Amberleigh—were safe, too. They might be Brody's, but she cared about them. They'd been in harm's way today, just like Cal.

And Brody. Everything about Brody. He'd been incredible. So strong, so fast, so damn capable. He'd taken control before she'd realized what had happened. What *could* have happened.

She pressed her eyes shut and leaned against the stall's wall.

It was okay. And now that it was over and everything *was* going to be okay, she didn't need to fall apart. But she was. Right here, right now, in a bathroom stall of the Soda Shop.

Sobs racked her, loud and pathetic. Every time she felt like she was getting control of her life, something knocked her feet out from under her. And this time it wasn't a something, it was a someone. Brody. Not that it was his fault. It was her own traitorous heart.

No, not her heart. She couldn't let him in her heart. Her heart had nothing to do with this. It was about being lonely, that was all. She hiccupped, more tears streaming down her cheeks.

"India?" Mrs. Wallace spoke softly.

She'd been crying too loudly to hear the woman come into the bathroom? Which meant Mrs. Wallace was fully aware of her meltdown.

"Are you all right? Can I help?" The sincere concern in the woman's voice only made it worse.

"I—I'm fine," she managed.

"No, dear, you're not," she argued gently, knocking on the stall door. "Come on out, now. It's not that bad, surely."

It was. It really was. And it reaffirmed the need to get out of Fort Kyle as soon as possible. She had to— she could not fall for Brody Wallace. Maybe this idea to see where their attraction would take them wasn't such a good idea after all.

"India, please," Ramona Wallace said. "I remember when Brody was real little. He got pneumonia and ended up in the hospital. I was so strong for him, of course. But I cried buckets whenever I was alone. Even after the doctors assured me he'd be just fine, I cried. From relief then, I guess." She paused. "Today was a shock, I'm sure. But your boy is fine—"

"And the girls." Her voice cracked.

"Oh, India, yes, they are right as rain. Right now, your boy is telling stories and making them all smile. He is a downright delight."

India smiled, wiping tears from her cheeks.

"I can't imagine how hard it must be, on your own. Times like this must be especially hard. Having friends is a great comfort." She paused. "Friends like Brody?"

Brody. Her heart was beating again, rapidly.

"Come on out, India," she repeated.

India wiped her face and opened the stall door. "I'm sorry. I just… I knew I was going to cry and didn't want to upset the kids."

"That's very thoughtful of you." Mrs. Wallace nodded. "Better now?"

"I think so," she admitted, washing her face and hands.

"Can I ask you a question?" Mrs. Wallace leaned against the bathroom counter. "You and Brody were in school together here, weren't you?"

She dried her hands and face with paper towels and glanced at the woman. "We knew each other." What was Mrs. Wallace looking for?

Her gaze was tawny, almost gold, like her granddaughters and her son. And equally intense. "Were you friends?"

India hesitated, but then nodded, smiling softly. "Yes, ma'am. Brody was a good friend…one of the few people I could count on back then."

"Was he?" she asked, offering India a tissue. Where

had that smile come from? And what did it mean? "Well, I should get back to Brody and the girls," she said, patting India's hand before she left the bathroom.

India washed her face again, ignored her reflection and returned to the table. To find Jan Ramirez in her seat.

"Oh, did I take your seat?" the woman asked, smiling up at her.

"No, not at all," India said. "Cal and I were just leaving." She took care not to look Brody's way. If she was lucky, she might just be able to keep herself together.

"Your truck is still at the fort," Brody said. "I can drive you two back to the fort—"

"It's okay," she said, smiling at Cal. "I bet Tandy can give us a ride when she's done."

Cal smiled back. "Think I can see Tanner again?"

"We'll have to see what she says." She prayed her cousin was still at the clinic. Her phone, her purse, everything but her keys, were still in the truck at the fort. "Let's head that way."

"Cal is leaving?" Suellen asked.

"No horny toads?" Amberleigh asked.

"Not today," Mrs. Wallace said. "But I'm sure we can try again soon."

"When Tanner is better." Cal nodded. "See you soon, Brody? For lessons?"

India squeezed Cal's hand. "Oh, Cal, I think Brody's too busy for that."

"Not at all," Brody said. "We should get started soon so you can ride in the cattle drive."

He was using Cal to bait her. And it was working. If she said no now she'd be the one to lose out—disappointing Cal and crushing his excitement.

"Brody's going to teach you to ride?" Mrs. Wallace

asked. "He's a good rider, Cal. Every Texas boy should know how to ride."

"Yes, ma'am," Cal agreed. "If I'm good enough, maybe my papa will let me ride in the cattle drive."

"I'm sure he will," Mrs. Wallace said. "I think I might have one of Brody's old saddles, too. Might help you sit better."

India couldn't help but look at Mrs. Wallace in disbelief. As nice as this was, why was she acting like this? She was a Wallace—Cal was a Boone. If anyone was aware of the feud, Ramona Wallace surely was.

She glanced at Brody then, relieved to see he was just as confused as she was. Once his tawny eyes locked with hers, she tore her attention from him. Her control was in short supply.

"We'll see," she said, refusing to be cornered on this.

"I'll call you later," Brody said, equally determined.

"Thank you, Brody," Cal said, pulling free of her hold to run to Brody. He hugged the man, a long, tight hug. "And thank you for taking care of Tanner. You saved him like he saved us." His little voice broke.

Brody's arms wrapped around her son so he could hug the boy tight. "You can count on me, Cal."

Brody Wallace had no right to say things like that to her son. Or to her. Damn him and his promises—promises she knew he'd keep. India felt them again—hot, burning tears—singeing the back of her eyelids. She was not going to cry now. Not when Jan Ramirez was analyzing every single thing that was happening. She waited, holding herself rigid, until Cal was holding her hand and tugging her toward the door of the Soda Shop. And even though she knew Brody was watching her, she didn't turn back—but she thought about it more than once.

WHEN INDIA AND Cal left, his mother bundled the girls up and headed home. Though Jan had offered to come back another day, Brody was determined to get this done and over with. He and Jan hit every major historical and tourist spot in the region before heading to his place for iced tea on the front porch.

When the WQAI van drove away from his house later that evening, Brody was ready for some peace and quiet. By then, he knew Jan Ramirez was hunting for something specific—and it had nothing to do with his run for office and everything to do with him and India.

India.

He was worried about her. Watching her come back to the table with tear-stained cheeks had been a punch to the gut. But then Cal had hugged him, and his heart turned over. Her boy clung to him, so full of love to give it damn near choked Brody up. He'd teach that boy to ride, no matter how hard India might fight him.

If India wasn't so hell-bent on leaving, he could imagine a future full of walks, special walks, hidden smiles and that thrum of excitement only India stirred. He felt more awake, more alive, when she was with him.

But he'd have to be careful. Apparently he was wearing his heart on his sleeve, and people like Jan Ramirez were far too observant not to notice. His interview went well. He'd talked the talk, remained charming and engaging and given her exactly what she'd said she wanted—an inside scoop on him. India wasn't part of the deal. Before Jan left, he made her swear not to include any footage of India or Cal in her reports. She'd been surprised, but she'd agreed.

"Willie called," his father said, phone in hand. "Seems the grocery store roof is leaking. Probably from the storm."

"Bad?" he asked.

"Sounds like it." His father sighed. "You know Willie."

Brody grinned. "Still got a few hours of light left. I'll head into town and check it out."

"Good." His father nodded. "Make sure he's got those wet-floor signs up, too, so no one falls and breaks a hip. Don't want to get sued."

"Yes, sir," he said.

"The girls are down?" his father asked.

"Yep." He had no idea what his mother had told him, so he said, "It was an eventful day."

"Amberleigh said ya'll were looking for a baby dragon?" His father scratched his head. "She does know they're not real, doesn't she?"

"She's a little girl, Dad. It's not gonna hurt a thing for her to believe in something make-believe," he countered. "She'll grow up soon enough."

"I guess." His father shook his head. "You were never one for pretending."

Brody didn't disagree. His parents were practical, hardworking people. Things like bedtime stories and playing pretend didn't always fit into their schedules— or their way of thinking. He understood that now. His father taught him to hunt and fish, how to fix a tractor engine, everything there was to know about taking care of your horse, things that would serve him well if he was ever stranded far from civilization. Dragons and fairies, mermaids and dinosaurs weren't included.

"You need anything else?" he asked, heading toward his truck. "Let Mom know I'm heading into town. She'll text me."

He enjoyed the twenty-five minutes of quiet into town—not even bothering to turn on the radio. He loved his girls and was thankful for his parents. But people needed time alone with their thoughts. Especially after a day like today.

His thoughts wandered to the girls' birthday, the campaign and festival, and then the holidays not too far after. What would the holidays look like? Would Barbara want the girls, or would she come to Fort Kyle so they could be together? Whatever it was, they'd make it work.

Cal sprang to mind then.

What sort of man abandoned his son? Three years. He couldn't imagine going three days without his girls.

He drove down Main Street and parked behind the grocery store. He unlocked the crank on the ladder bolted to the building and extended it fully before carrying his flashlight to the top. A quick search showed a soft patch in the corner, made worse by the slight incline in the flat roof. The water had pooled there instead of running off via the drains. He sighed, ran his hand over his face and shook his head.

His father was going to have to spend some money on this. Which meant Brody would have to smooth ruffled feathers.

He stood, staring down on Main Street. It was getting dark. The old-fashioned streetlights came on, casting the wood and brick storefronts in welcoming halos. The faint strands of music from the Soda Shop jukebox spilled into the night. His home was a pretty little town—even prettier in the fading sunlight.

He took a few pictures of the roof with his cell phone and climbed back down the ladder.

He unlocked the back door of the grocery store and went looking for Willie. Once he'd filled the man in on his discovery, and made sure the area was marked off, he headed across the street for a cup of black coffee.

But seeing India sitting at the desk inside the antiques

shop, her sloppy bun stuck through with a handful of pencils, changed his mind.

He took a deep breath and tested the front door. It was unlocked. "India?" he said.

Her head jerked up, sending two pencils flying. She reached up, tugging the rest out and rubbing the back of her head.

"Studying?" he asked.

She nodded.

"Didn't mean to interrupt you." Which was a lie. If he hadn't wanted to interrupt her, why the hell had he walked into the shop?

"No more camera crew?" she asked, tapping her book with her pencil.

"They left a couple hours back." He leaned against the counter and watched her reaction. "Not a fan of television?"

She had shadows beneath her eyes. "Not a fan of stirring up a hornet's nest. Rather not draw unwanted attention."

"Your dad?"

Her eyes met his. "And Cal's father. I like that he's gone. I'd like to keep it that way." She stood, agitated.

"Is Cal here?" he asked.

She seemed to be considering her answer. "Spending the night with Click and Tandy. We wanted to cheer Cal up, try to keep him from worrying over Tanner. Now he's all fired up about riding and horses." She shot him a look.

"I'm glad he's excited. He should be." He wasn't going to apologize for it.

She sighed. "We'll see."

Brody tipped his hat back on his head. "What happened? With your ex?"

She shook her head. "I'm not in the mood to talk about

JT. The only thing good that came out of my marriage was Cal. And the realization that the only person I can really count on is myself."

"What about your family?" he argued.

"You know it's never been easy between me and my father. Marrying JT was the last straw. Dad never liked him. He was right not to. Now he barely speaks to me. I'm an embarrassment." She glanced at him. "Sorry. Today was a lot. Guess I'm still a little worked up."

He hurt for her. Surely it wasn't true. Woodrow Boone was a hard man, but how could he be ashamed of his daughter? Not want her close by? "That why you're so determined to get out of here?"

"Would you stay someplace you weren't wanted? Where you had to be reminded all the time of your mistakes?"

His heart sank. "I guess talking to your dad is out?"

Her smile was hard. "He's made up his mind. He was right. I was wrong. He told me what to do and I didn't listen—making my situation my fault. When I called him, asked him for help, he reminded me of that." She broke off. "I came back because I had no place to go. I didn't want to, but I did—for Cal. And when I'm ready, I'll be taking Cal and starting out fresh, away from my dad's judgment."

Brody nodded. "My dad's never going to forget I left Fort Kyle. Not ever. I don't think there's a thing I can do to fix it—to make him think I didn't desert him somehow."

India frowned. "I don't want to do that to Cal. Hold on to things, hold mistakes over him. I want him to know I'm always here for him, no matter what. No judgment or conditions or guilt."

"I'll shake to that," he said, offering her his hand.

She laughed, eyeing his hand before taking it. Watching her smile was a thing of wonder. Her smile washed over him like a ray of sunshine, blinding and brilliant.

He pulled her into his arms. "You're beautiful, India." He shook his head.

Her smile softened, the pain in her eyes fading.

"And you're an incredible mother. Cal is proof of that." He liked the way her cheeks turned pink, the shy smile his praise caused. "If no one has told you, you're doing a great job with him."

"You're being awfully charming again, Brody Wallace." He liked the waver in her voice, uncertain and sweet.

He nuzzled her temple. "Could be I'm just being honest."

She shook her head, her words soft and low. "I know charm when I hear it. JT was a charmer. Since he left me scarred inside and out, I can't help but be suspicious of it."

His brain short-circuited when she'd mentioned JT. *Scarred. Inside and out.* The bastard had laid hands on her? Hurt her? He was frozen, his hands stiff against her and his heart thumping in his chest. His anger with her ex gave way to something sharper, something crushing. His arms tightened around her, pulling her flush against him, as if he could protect her now…from her past.

"I don't want to think about my father or JT or anything else." She looked up at him. "I want you to kiss me until nothing else matters."

The hunger in her gaze was for him. This was what she wanted. So this was what he'd give her. His lips brushed across hers, featherlight and teasing. Her hands fisted in his shirt, pulling him closer. He smiled against her lips, his mouth sealed firmly with hers.

"Then, that's what I'll do," he said simply. His lips

brushed hers once again. His tongue stroked deep, and she moaned, her fingers tugging his hair.

Their rapid breathing filled the room.

He bit back a groan. She was so damn soft pressed against him. His hands explored, stroking over the thin fabric of her shirt to feel the heat of her skin beneath his fingertips. Her scent was a jolt to the senses. He'd never wanted anything the way he wanted India Boone. Having her in his arms was beyond anything he could ever have imagined. He was holding her, but she was the one in control. He loved her, but she didn't want his love right now. She wanted his body—and he'd give it to her.

He was, without a doubt, completely under her power.

Chapter Eleven

His hand cradled her cheek. His golden eyes had her trapped, and she liked it. India held on to Brody with everything she had. His kiss was all-consuming, soft yet firm, tender but fierce, flooding her with want. When his tongue touched hers, her fingers gripped his shirtfront for support. She wanted his lips on hers, wanted his fingers sliding through her hair and pressing her tightly against him. Being in his arms chased away everything else.

His touch made it okay to forget—for now.

His mouth traveled along her jaw to the sensitive skin behind her ear, then along her neck. One big, strong hand pressed flat against her back. The other cradled her cheek in his palm, his thumb leaving a scorching trail in its wake. When his lips traveled to the base of her throat, he paused, his breath harsh and ragged against her skin.

She liked being tangled up in him. Liked the feel of his heart pounding beneath her palm. Everything about this was right. When their eyes locked, the raw hunger in his golden gaze had the last vestiges of her control falling away.

She didn't want control or thought, practicality or reason. She wanted this man, desperately. Wanted him like air. Now. Her hunger was new and raw and slightly unnerving.

His lips lifted. "India?" His hold eased, giving them room to breathe.

She drew in a deep breath, almost groaning as his scent flooded her nose and lungs. "I just... This is... A lot."

He grinned, his thumb brushing over her lower lip.

She shuddered at the featherlight touch, need setting her blood on fire. "Maybe too much?"

His gaze traveled over her face, the corners of his mouth turning up. "You're saying I'm too much for you?"

Her laugh was breathy. "I'm saying I don't know what to do with this." Her hands tightened on his shirtfront, making her even more aware of the rock-hard chest beneath the neatly pressed shirt. "With you."

He nodded. "What do you want to do?" he asked, his voice gruff and pitched low.

A dozen possibilities played through her mind. But none of them was acceptable to say out loud. Her experience with JT hadn't provided a foundation for what was happening between her and Brody. Nothing had prepared her for this. She wanted Brody, to touch him and kiss him and explore the contours of his body. She wanted him to keep looking at her like he was now—like there was no place else he'd rather be.

"This. You. I want you to take me home," she murmured. "And I want you to stay."

His jaw tightened. "You're sure?"

She nodded. "Absolutely."

He frowned. "It's been a hell of a day, India. We don't need to rush things."

"You're right," she agreed. "But there's no rush. Tonight, we can be like we were. You and me." She smiled. "Talking. Laughing. Us against the world."

"I can do that, Goldilocks." He smiled down at her, his arms sliding from her waist. "Whenever you're ready."

She was more than ready. But they still had to get the Fire Gorge work truck from the fort before they could head home. "I'll hurry," she said, slipping from his hold to close the shop.

"What can I do?" he asked.

"Check and make sure the back door is locked?" she asked, straightening up the desk, filing the few invoices away and packing up her things onto the bookcase behind the counter.

He returned. "All locked up."

"Thanks." She stood, pushed her chair in and turned off the desk light.

"My pleasure," he said, at her back. His hands settled at her waist as his nose ran along the curve of her neck. He kissed the skin behind her ear and released her. "Anything else?"

"Eager to leave?" Her voice wobbled. She heard it. He probably heard it, too.

"Hell, yes." He took her hand in his, threading their fingers together as he led her toward the shop door.

He released her when they were outside, but India didn't let it get to her. They both needed to be careful—for different reasons. They got into his truck.

"I need to let Scarlett know not to come get me," she said once they were on the road. She typed in a quick text, Got a ride home. See you tomorrow. Then hit Send.

Scarlett's response was quick. With who? Followed by a string of smiling emojis and hearts.

India giggled. Nothing to tell.

"What?" Brody asked.

"My sister," she said, taking his hand in hers. "She's a hopeless romantic."

"That's bad?" he asked.

"It's…unrealistic. A recipe for disaster. Scarlett's so gentle, I worry about her. I'm afraid her first heartbreak might really break her heart." She tucked her phone back into her pocket. "We should get the ranch truck. Dad will notice if it's missing."

They drove to the fort, shared a handful of stolen kisses and drove the remaining leg of their journey apart. She held her breath as she parked at the truck shed and Brody kept going. It was late, and her parents were probably in bed in their bedroom that was on the other side of the property—ensuring her comings and goings were nobody else's business but her own.

She walked along the path to her cabin. Tanner was always with her, chasing away any threat the wide-open spaces and thick black of night might offer. But now, without him at her side, she walked a little faster.

Brody's truck was parked behind the cabin, but he sat on the front porch, waiting for her.

"Any trouble?" he asked, his hand low on her back as she unlocked her door.

"No." She closed the door and stared up at him. The look on his face tore at her heart. "What's wrong?"

He took her hands in his. "I was thinking about what you said—about Scarlett. It got me thinking. Is that what happened with you?"

"What did I say?" The whole drive here she'd been thinking about being back in his arms.

"Did JT break your heart?" he asked, his hand squeezing hers.

She stared at their hands, his words ringing in her ears. "Why is this so important to you?"

His fingers brushed along her jaw. "I've known you most of my life, Goldilocks. Something happened to plant doubt in your eyes—doubt that wasn't there before. I want to know how it got there so I can help get it out."

She stared at him, the thump of her heart heavy and slow.

"It matters," he said. "To me, it matters."

Had JT broken her heart? "By the time he left, my heart had already healed." She would have paced the tiny room, but he caught her hand and pulled her into the circle of his arms. "I thought I loved him. He was very good at figuring out how to charm people—like a chameleon. And, boy, could he work a room. People bought in even though JT had no plans to make any of it happen. Things fell apart. He fell apart. Our marriage did, too." She shook her head. "And once I knew what he was capable of... I knew it was all a lie."

Brody cleared his throat. "He... Did he hurt you?"

India stared up at his face then. She'd never told anyone what had happened between her and JT. It pressed in on her some nights, creeping into her dreams and pulling her from a dead sleep sweating and crying and shaking with fear. Some things changed the way other people would look at her. But not Brody. Maybe telling him would make it easier to bear. "He did. But I made sure he never hurt Cal."

Brody made an odd noise in the back of his throat but didn't say a word. He sat on the lumpy, overstuffed couch and pulled her into his lap. She stayed cradled close for a long time, the beat of his heart beneath her ear.

"Brody?" she whispered, hoping she hadn't made a terrible mistake.

"Give me a minute." He smoothed the hair from her forehead and pressed a kiss to her temple.

But the silence stretched on until she couldn't take it. She should have kept her mouth shut, brushed his question aside and kept things light. Maybe there were some things no one wanted to hear. But sitting here in silence wasn't going to help. So she asked the questions that she'd had since seeing him again. "What about you? You and the girls' mother."

"Barbara? We're good friends. I don't think either one of us was too heartbroken." He chuckled, his hold easing slightly. "Guess that means neither of us was fully invested. I get the girls eighty percent of the time—thanks to her career."

But there was no malice in his voice. That was who Brody was, accepting and honest. He didn't hold grudges. Or jump to conclusions. He didn't say anything he didn't mean. And he was unfailingly loyal.

"Considering how things could have turned out, I'd say I'm lucky," he murmured.

She didn't argue, but she knew the truth. Brody's ex-wife had been the lucky one. She'd had this man's devotion, his love and their family. She'd let it all go. Brody deserved a woman who'd fight for him and his girls. Someone who'd never let them go.

But tonight, he was hers.

His big hands stroked along her back, up her neck and through her hair. She closed her eyes, reveling in the way he held her—the way he touched her. She shuddered and nuzzled closer to press her lips to his throat. Her lips traveled up his neck, along his jaw, and sucked his earlobe into her mouth, dragging a broken curse from his lips. The taste of him, salt and man and fresh air, was pure intoxication.

Her hands tightened on his shoulders as she moved to kiss him. He groaned against her lips, his hands fisting in the back of her shirt as he crushed her against him. But it wasn't enough.

BRODY HAD ALWAYS prided himself on keeping a clear head. But India was challenging that. It wasn't just her kisses or eager touches, it was her abandon. There was an urgency to her he understood. The pull between them was hot and demanding. And when her lips sealed with his, he was pulled under.

His hands slid beneath her shirt, her skin silk beneath his touch. His fingers ran along her sides, drawing a shudder from her—making her arch into him. Damn but she was soft. And sweet.

Her fingers fell to the buttons on his shirt, freeing the fabric and tugging the shirt wide. She tore her lips from his to look at his chest. But he wasn't sure what she was thinking, good or bad, until her fingers began a feather-light exploration of his bare skin.

"We had gym together," she murmured, smiling. "This is all new."

He chuckled, shrugging out of his shirt and tossing it on the chair across the room. "Guess I was a late bloomer."

Her eyes met his, blazing—wanting—making his body hard for her.

He reached for her, his hands cradling her face as he kissed her. Softly at first, gently. But that apparently wasn't enough for India. Her fingers twined into his hair. She arched into him, pressing the swell of her breasts against his chest. She wanted more, and he would give it to her.

He nipped her lower lip, exploring the rounded contour with his tongue and teeth while his hand slid up, brushing between her shoulder blades. A gasp parted her lips and gave his tongue access. The heat of her mouth and sweep of her tongue was the last coherent thought he had. On and on it went, her lips fastened to his. Her hands sliding over his chest so she could wrap her arms around him.

One second she was holding him close, the next she was pushing away—and pulling her shirt up and over her head. He watched, mesmerized by the display before him. A lacy peach bra covered her breasts. The scrap of fabric was more modest than most bikini tops, but it was the sexiest damn thing he'd ever seen in his life.

Made even sexier by how fast she wriggled out of it.

And still, all he could do was stare at the gift she was giving him.

"Damn, Goldilocks. You're so beautiful." He ran his fingers along her temple and into her long blond hair.

She smiled, a blush stealing across her cheeks as she leaned into him, the shock of being skin to skin emptying his lungs. And when his hand cradled the full weight of her breast, he was gasping for breath again. She moaned at the brush of his thumb against her nipple. Her eyes fluttered shut when his mouth and tongue explored the sensitive tip. "Brody," she whispered.

His name from her lips had him aching. He kissed her again, crushing her against him as he lay back against the couch.

"Ow." She arched up. "Ow," she repeated.

He pushed off her.

She sat up and pushed on the couch. "Damn spring."

Damn spring or no, there was no denying he had one hell of a view. She was frowning, breathing heavy, lips swollen from his kisses, with her hair falling around her full breasts.

"You okay?" he asked.

She stood, took his hand and led him into the next room. Her bedroom. She cast a quick glance his way.

"You said you wanted me to hold you, India." He tilted her head back. "That's all I want."

She bit her lip, her gaze sweeping over his chest and face. "It's not all I want. I mean, I do, want that…but now…" She paused, stepping closer to him. "I've never felt this before, Brody. Never ached like this."

How the hell was he supposed to argue with that? And what the hell sort of man had JT been? India was a passionate woman. She'd come alive under his touch, giving pleasure and taking pure, unfiltered joy in receiving it. That he made her feel something she'd never felt before was a gift he wasn't going to take for granted. He did that. And they were just getting started.

She shimmied out of her jeans before he realized what she was doing.

He swallowed, studying every inch of her. The swell of her breasts, the curve of her hips and the dip of her waist. She was beyond imagination. This was the woman he'd always loved. And now she wanted him.

As soon as he'd kicked off his boots, jeans and boxers, he scooped her up and laid her back on the bed. He could have stared at her all night, but she gripped his arms and tugged him down on top of her. The bed squeaked and dipped.

"Careful." He laughed, bracing himself before he squished her.

She laughed, too, her hands reaching up to cradle his face.

He shook his head, loving her laugh, loving her smile and the spark in her gaze. He bent to kiss her, the fire between them burning bright. He was throbbing with want. And love. Damn but he loved this woman.

"You're beautiful India," he whispered.

"So are you." She smiled as she tugged him down to

kiss her. He was happy to oblige. His lips and tongue trailed from her lips to her neck, her neck to her shoulder, and her shoulder to the valley between her breasts. He wanted to take his time and learn every inch of her. But the urgency between them was undeniable. And when he sucked one pebbled nipple into his mouth, her fingertips bit into his hips and pulled him close.

He moaned when her legs parted for him. And when he was buried deep inside her he moaned again. This time, so did she. It was more than he could ever have anticipated. Every thrust was a shock, blindingly hot and intense. Being one, lost in her, felt right.

Her head fell back, a blissful smile on her face, as she held on to him. He watched, marveling at the shift of emotions on her face. She was lost in this—in them. Her hands roamed his body. The rasp of her breath fanned against his chest. She hooked a leg around his waist and arched to meet him. And fell instantly apart. Her cry was soft—almost surprised—as her body tightened around him.

His climax followed hers, sending wave after wave of pure pleasure crashing into him again and again. His moan tore from his throat, stealing all the air in his lungs and leaving him drained.

He was gasping when he opened his eyes to stare down at her.

Her arm was thrown over her eyes, a huge smile on her face.

"All good?" he asked, smiling as her arm moved away and she stared up at him.

"Incredible," she whispered. "That was…wow. I've never… I mean, yes, very good."

He frowned. "Never what?"

She shook her head, still smiling. "Kiss me." Her arms twined around his neck.

"I could kiss you all night, Goldilocks," he whispered, kissing her softly.

Her sigh was so sweet, his heart was happy. He'd done this to her, made her moan with pleasure and sigh with satisfaction. He'd happily do it again. Especially if what she'd almost said meant what he thought it meant. India had never had an orgasm. How was that possible? Tonight had proved how ardent a lover she was. If he hadn't known her ex-husband was a selfish bastard, this would have told him all he needed to know about the man.

India needed a man who would treat her—mind and body—as the treasure she was. And, damn, but he wanted to be that man.

Chapter Twelve

Indie's eyes popped open, her cheek on Brody's chest and her arm draped across his waist. She smiled, stretched and eased closer. As tempting as it was to wake him again, she knew they were playing with fire.

A glance at the clock had her bolting upright.

"Brody." She shook him.

"India," he groaned. "A man's got to sleep."

She burst out laughing. "No. Not…that. It's almost five."

His eyes opened, a slow smile forming. "Five, huh?" He shook his head. "I don't know if I can move."

She laughed again. "You better. For your personal safety." Her smile faded somewhat. Her father could not see him here now—leaving her place. "What were we thinking?" she asked, panic threatening her earlier happiness.

He sat up, cupping her cheek. "I was thinking how damn lucky I am to make you scream my name."

Her cheeks grew hot. She had, too. With great enthusiasm. He'd loved it. So had she. Her chest grew heavy and her body warmed at the thought. "Stop," she whispered. "You need to go."

He grinned. "I do. As tempting as it is to stay here and do it again, I value my life." He shook his head.

She nodded. "So do I."

"Good to know you're not just after my body." He winked, slipping to the edge of the bed.

Any rational person would be throwing clothes at him and hurrying him along, but…India didn't move. She was too content to watch him. He had an incredible body—just as she'd suspected. Lean muscles and boundless energy had combined for the most incredible night of her life. And…her first orgasm. Which led to many more.

She smiled.

"What?" he asked, buttoning his jeans.

"Nothing." She needed to stop smiling.

Hands on hips, brows raised, he waited. "That smile means something." He grinned. "Something good, I'd think."

She hugged her knees to her chest and tugged up her sheet.

"You're going to get modest now?" He shook his head. "I admit, I'm a fan of wild and demanding India—"

"I was not demanding," she argued, her cheeks hot.

"I hate to argue with you, Goldilocks, but you were." He leaned forward to kiss her on the forehead. "And I liked it."

He was right. Last night, she'd been a woman possessed. Something about Brody flipped a switch on her libido. Like now. She grabbed him, rising up on her knees to kiss him.

He moaned, crawling onto the bed to pull her flush against him. "I can stay a little longer."

As much as she wanted him to stay, right here, in her bed, she knew better. "You have three little girls who expect to see their father when they wake up," she said between kisses. Her father's anger she could deal with if she had to, but she wouldn't keep little girls from their dad.

She let go of him, pushing against his chest. "You can't stay." She cast one last look at his incredible chest and slid off the other side of the bed. She wrapped the sheet around her and headed into the kitchen to collect his shirt.

He followed, taking his shirt from her and sliding it on. "I'll see you later on, with Cal? We'll get his lessons started this afternoon at Click's place."

"I'm still not sure that's a good idea," she argued.

"You weren't sure last night was a good idea, either." He grinned. "It turned out pretty well, I'm thinking."

How could he do that? Make her cheeks—and her body—burn with a simple grin?

He pulled her into his arms. "Making you come apart for the first time was one of the greatest gifts I've been given." He kissed her. "Glad we didn't stop at just once, though. You know, practice is always a good thing."

She was too breathless to argue. There was no point in arguing. He was right. About everything. Instead she kissed him back, breaking off to say, "I'm now a fan of practice."

He kissed her again. "I'll make sure we get more practice time, Goldilocks, don't you worry."

"I'll hold you to that." With a final kiss, she stepped out of his arms. "Now get out of here before my daddy shoots you."

Brody laughed. "Last night might have been worth it." He winked and opened the door. But he hesitated on the front porch, shooting her a look she wasn't prepared for. It wasn't just attraction in his tawny gaze. No, it was more. It seeped into her slowly and cradled her heart in tenderness. "You're beautiful."

She leaned against the porch railing and watched him drive away. Even after he was gone, she stood, watching the sun break over the horizon.

The enormity of last night hit her. She had slept with Brody Wallace. She closed her eyes, flashes of their night together warming her through and through. She'd loved every minute of their time together. No one had ever treated her like that—like her pleasure mattered. Like he was honored to be with her.

Now that he was gone, there was nothing to chase away the fear and panic that clawed its way from her stomach to her throat.

Yes, there would be hell to pay if people found out. But…that wasn't it. There was this very real, very intense, very undeniable sense that Brody hadn't just introduced her to pleasure. He might have introduced her to something so much more…

"CAL AND TANNER?" Amberleigh said as soon as Brody opened his eyes.

"What?" he asked, peering at the clock on his bedside table. It was six thirty. He'd driven home, taken a shower, fallen into bed, and thirty minutes later all three of his girls had climbed into bed to stare at him. Today was going to be rough. But damn it was worth it.

"Tanner okay?" Suellen asked.

"Go see him?" Marilyn asked.

He yawned, rubbing a hand over his face. "Not today, girls. Tanner probably won't be going home for a bit. And then he'll need lots of rest." Not three rambunctious toddlers nursing him back to health.

Three identical frowns creased his daughters' faces.

He flopped back on the pillows. "Maybe later."

He dozed while they played princess ponies in his bed. But once Amberleigh declared she was hungry, he knew it was time to get up.

"Pancakes? After you get dressed," he said, shooing them from his room long enough to get dressed himself.

His mother was already in the kitchen. "Good morning," she said, planting a kiss on his cheek. "You sleep well? You came in late." Her voice lowered, but he heard her say, "Or, should I say, early?" And, judging from the look she shot him, she wasn't happy about it.

"I think I'm a little old for you to be keeping tabs on me, Mom." He smiled at her.

"You'll always be my boy, Brody. As long as you're under this roof, I'll be keeping tabs on you." She shook her head. "I was thinking about India Boone and her boy, Cal."

Brody stopped assembling cups with screw-on lids and straws and looked at his mother. He knew she'd followed India into the bathroom at the Soda Shop—he was glad she had. His mother was good at saying, or not saying, what needed to be said. But he couldn't shake the feeling that she was getting at something. "What about them?"

"You should invite them to the girls' birthday party," she said. "The girls adore him. And, I think, she's fond of you and the girls. And, maybe, you're fond of her... them?"

He saw her quick look his way but didn't quite know what to make of it.

"What do you think?" she asked.

"I think Dad would blow a gasket." He went back to pouring milk and screwing on the lids.

His mother flipped a pancake and crossed her arms, looking at him. "Well, that's nonsense." She sighed. "Your father loves those girls and wants them happy. I'll talk to him."

"You don't have to, Mom. Even if Dad is okay with it, I don't think her dad would be. The two of them bump heads enough without adding her partying on enemy territory." He collected all three cups and carried them to the table, where the girls waited.

"You seem to know an awful lot about her," his mother said, serving each girl a pancake.

Brody used the pizza cutter to cut each pancake into little bite-size pieces, hoping to avoid further conversation about what he did or didn't know about India. And, if he didn't watch himself, she'd figure out just why he was coming home so early this morning. And why he'd spent the few minutes he'd had before his daughters' arrival hoping Tanner would recover—Cal needed him to.

"Brody?" His mother nudged him. "Amberleigh asked very nicely for syrup."

Brody poured a dollop of syrup onto Amberleigh's pancake. "Good job using your manners," he said, smiling at her.

"Where's your head this morning, boy?" his father said, joining them at the table.

Brody looked at his mother, surprised by the smile on her face. What was she up to?

"He's got a lot weighing on him," his mother said to his father, squeezing Vic's shoulder. "Doesn't look like he got much sleep last night, either."

"No? Like what?" his father asked.

"Nothing. I'm fine," he assured his father, his eyes on his plate. Yep, his mother was definitely up to something. "Plans today? I've got a quick meeting at the library at one. Can't imagine it'll take too long since I'm running unopposed. After that, I thought I'd take the girls out to Click's place—see all the horses." He took the plate of bacon his mother offered him.

"Don't forget your old saddle for Cal," she whispered. "It's in the back of the barn, in an old burlap feed sack."

"What?" his father barked.

"Just asking if he wanted sausage, too," his mother spoke up.

"Well, maybe I want sausage." His father frowned.

She laughed. "Of course you do."

"Paw-paw's yummies," Suellen said, grinning at her granddad.

"That's right." His father patted her cheek. "I love sausage."

"I thought it was off-limits?" Brody asked, shooting a look at his mother. The doctor had provided them with a list of things his father should not be eating. "I'm pretty sure bacon was on that list, too."

His father frowned. "You can't expect me to give up bacon and sausage. I'm a Texan, boy. I need meat at every meal. And when I say meat, I don't mean grilled chicken." He looked disgusted.

Brody bit back a laugh, shaking his head. His father would do what he pleased—he always had. Hell, between his father and the girls, this election and India, Brody had very little control in his life. He sat back in his chair and watched the interactions around the table. Nothing like having his family around him to remind him how lucky he was. His family might not agree on everything, but there was love here. The girls were chattering, eating up their breakfasts, all smiles and carefree. His father, grumbles aside, looked good. His color was less blotchy, and for the most part, his temper was in check. And his mother. Even if she was watching him with that small knowing smile on her face.

"What?" he asked.

Her brows rose. "What do you mean *what*?" She sipped her orange juice. "I was just thinking about the girls and their new friend. How they get on so well."

Brody scowled.

"Cal?" Amberleigh piped up. "Cal's my friend."

"Poor Cal and Tanner." Marilyn sighed, her little face drooping.

"Tanner's better," Suellen jumped in. "Doc said so."

"Who is Tanner?" his father asked. "Are we talking about Cal Boone again? You seem to be spending a lot of a time with that Boone girl and her boy."

"Friends," Amberleigh said.

"Yup." Suellen nodded.

"Poor Tanner." Marilyn sighed again.

"Who is Tanner?" his father asked again.

"Cal's dog. He saved the girls from a copperhead yesterday," his mother said. "But the poor dog was bitten in the process."

His father stared at them. "And no one thought to mention this to me?"

"Everyone is fine. There's no need getting worked up over what could have happened." His mother smiled at him.

"Poor Tanner," Marilyn mourned.

"Is the dog dead?" his father asked, frowning.

Brody shook his head. "No. He might lose an eye. But that's it."

"Hmm," his father said, nodding. "Sounds like a damn good dog."

"Damn good," Amberleigh repeated with feeling.

Brody was stunned silent by Amberleigh's earnest declaration. She didn't know better. But his parents did. His mother was covering her mouth with a napkin, but he could tell she was smiling. And his father? His father was laughing so hard tears were pouring down his face.

And that, right there, was enough to let Amberleigh's bad word slide—this time.

Chapter Thirteen

India headed to Click and Tandy's place as soon as she'd showered and had some coffee. Sitting here worrying over what she'd done, how she felt and whether or not it was all a mistake was pointless. But, without distraction, that was exactly what she'd do. Besides, she wanted to see Cal. She could count all the nights they'd spend apart on one hand.

"You're here bright and early." Tandy greeted her on the porch, coffee mug in hand. "In time for breakfast. Click's got Pearl and Cal helping him make biscuits."

India could only imagine Click and Tandy's toddler and Cal making biscuits. More likely they were making a mess. She smiled at the thought. "How'd it go?"

"Cal is good as gold, India. You know that. He's so sweet with Pearl." She smiled. "You look good—you're practically glowing this morning."

"Am I?" she asked, touching her cheek.

"You are." Tandy's eyes narrowed.

"I...I got some extra sleep," she lied.

"Oh?" Tandy asked. "Interesting. I thought maybe it had something to do with Brody Wallace taking you home last night?"

She stared at her cousin.

"Small town," Tandy said.

Her stomach sank. "Please tell me it was Scarlett and not Miss Francis? She'd have it all over—"

"No, no, it was Scarlett. I was teasing you, India. I'm sorry." Tandy took her hand. "I invited her out last night, and she said she had to pick you up. A few minutes later she said she was free because Brody was driving you." She frowned. "You look terrified."

"Hoping to avoid more drama with Dad. You know how big an ass he can be," she said.

Tandy nodded. "Why anyone feels like they need Woodrow Boone's approval is beyond me." She sighed. "Sorry. I know he's your father, but…"

"No apologies necessary." India smiled. Since Tandy's wedding her father had gone from downright cruel to brusquely civil toward Click Hale, who was the best kind of man. His love for Tandy and their daughter, Pearl, was testament to that fact. "It'd be easier if I wasn't having to rely on him right now." She shrugged. "Not that he'd ever be fine with my dating a Wallace, but at least it wouldn't be happening under his roof."

Tandy nodded. "Are you? Dating Brody?"

She smiled, bombarded by a flood of memories that made her stomach warm and fluid. "I'm not sure." She blew out a slow breath.

"He's one of the good ones," Tandy said. "No matter what your daddy might think."

"I know that." She nodded. "But, we don't make sense, Tandy. I have plans. Plans that give Cal and me a real future, you know? I just want to take care of my son—to give him a chance to grow up without all the drama and noise and…judgment." She sighed. "Falling for Brody and staying in Fort Kyle was never part of the plan."

"Falling…in love?" Tandy said.

India blinked, realizing too late what she'd said out loud. "No. I didn't mean—"

"Mom?" Cal asked, pushing through the front door. He grinned up at her. "You come for breakfast?"

"I did." She hugged him tight. "I heard you and Pearl were cooking. Couldn't miss out on that."

"Pearl's letting Banshee lick off the spoons," Cal said, laughing.

Banshee was Tandy's massive Anatolian shepherd. He was two-year-old Pearl's shadow, her canine nanny and watchdog rolled into one. A lot like Tanner was to Brody.

"Just tell me she's not putting the licked spoons back into the dough?" Tandy asked.

"Nope. Uncle Click's watching her." He grinned. "I should go help, though, 'cause she's really busy. You coming?"

"Yes, sir," she said, following her son inside, Tandy behind her.

Breakfast was a messy, laughter-filled event. Little Pearl, with her dimples and curly black hair, had her daddy wrapped around her little finger—as it should be.

While India and Tandy cleaned up the kitchen, Click offered to show her son the horses. "Already have the perfect horse picked out for you, Cal," he said. "Brody will get you riding like a professional in no time." He winked at her son, ruffling his hair and leading them to the barn.

India ignored the sharp tug on her heart. Did she really want Brody more involved in their lives? It ate at her to know her father couldn't find the time to take Cal riding—that her son wasn't a priority to him. Even if her dad could never forgive her for her past, there was no reason for him to treat Cal poorly. The more she thought about her father, the more upset she became.

Dammit, if Brody was willing to teach him to ride, she'd gladly accept.

"He was super excited about riding," Tandy said. "When he wasn't worrying over Tanner, he was listening to every piece of advice Click had for him." She looked at her. "You okay? You look a bit…riled up."

"I'm fine. Just indulging in a moment of self-pity." She did her best to brush aside her irritation, placing the mixing bowl she was drying on the dish rack. "I appreciate you two offering to keep Cal last night."

"We kept his mind off Tanner—for the most part. Click kept talking horses, and Pearl keeps everyone on their toes. I'd like to think he had a good time, too. It's good he's so interested in learning to ride. Riding, horses and cattle, being a cowboy—it's part of his heritage." Tandy glanced at her. "We can go get Tanner after his riding lesson? By then, I imagine Tanner will be champing at the bit to go home."

India smiled. "Sounds perfect. Thank you."

"I just did my job, India. You can thank Brody," she said. "If he hadn't been so quick, Tanner might not be doing so well."

Those words caused an ache in her heart. She and Cal loved Tanner. She was thankful Brody had been there. She was thankful for Brody… From his gentle, constant smile to his sturdy, reliable nature—Brody Wallace was the sort of man she wanted Cal to have in his life. A boy needed role models, men he could look up to, respect and emulate. If Cal's own grandfather wasn't up to the task while they were in town, she couldn't think of a better man than Brody to take her son under his wing.

And, if she allowed a moment's honesty with herself, she wanted Brody around. When he was with her, things didn't seem so big and overwhelming. He helped her set aside all the worrying and stressful thoughts of an unknown future and let her enjoy the here and now.

"India?" Tandy interrupted her thoughts. "I'm gonna put Pearl down for a nap. Heaven help us all. Pearl, the triplets and Cal on a horse. There hasn't been this much excitement in this house in a long time." She smiled, scooped up Pearl and headed down the hall to Pearl's nursery.

India finished cleaning up and walked out onto the back porch. From her vantage point, she could see Cal watching the horses. Standing on the lower rail with his arms draped over the top rail, he rested his chin on his hands. He was getting taller, growing every day—becoming more of a man with every second that ticked by. She needed to see that. Cal would never be this age again. She owed it to them both to give him her undivided time and attention now and then. Today was definitely one of those times. Even from here, she could tell her son was thrilled about today's adventure.

That Brody would be here only made things better.

"SHE'S RUNNING A FEVER," his mother said. "So is Suellen."

"Probably picked something up at the school." His father frowned. "Damn places are chock-full of germs." He couldn't stand the girls being sick. "Or that boy you're spending all that time with. He's older, isn't he? In school? He's carrying all sorts of sickness, I'll bet."

Leave it to his father to blame Cal Boone for his daughters' illness. Brody didn't say a word—to him. Instead, he smiled down at Suellen and Marilyn. "What hurts?"

"Here," Suellen said, pointing at her throat.

"Yep," Marilyn agreed. "Ow."

He sighed. "We'll call the doctor—"

"Call him?" His father was not pleased.

"It's the weekend, Dad. They're closed. I don't know if he does house calls—"

"He better get his ass out here to get them better now," his father huffed.

Brody frowned. "Dad?"

"What? They have a fever, boy." His dad was getting more worked up with each passing second. "What is it?" he asked his wife, who was holding the thermometer.

"One hundred degrees." She placed her hand on his arm. "Breathe, Vic, please. Kids have been getting sick and running temperatures forever. You don't need to get yourself all worked up—and neither do they," she added, her whisper surprisingly stern. "And no hovering, either. It's sure to put everyone on edge."

Vic frowned.

"Grumpy?" Amberleigh asked, frowning up at her grandfather.

His father burst out laughing. "Not grumpy, darling, worried. Your granddad doesn't like to see his girls under the weather is all."

Amberleigh laughed, too, patting her grandfather's hand in comfort. "It's okay."

It took a little more than an hour to get the doctor there and the girls medicated. Tonsillitis and ear infections. Soup, rest and medicine would have them right as rain by tomorrow.

Once the good doctor was on his way, his mother shooed them to the door. "You and Amberleigh go on, Brody. We'll get them soup and watch some princess movies on the couch. Best for Amberleigh, too. Might spare her from catching it."

"You're leaving?" His father stared at him like he'd grown another head.

"Vic." His mother shook her head. "You should go with Brody and Amberleigh." She nodded at him. "Go and help a little boy learn to ride a horse."

Brody froze. She could not be suggesting what he thought she was suggesting?

"What boy?" There was a razor-sharp edge to his father's voice. "You're leaving your sick daughters to help *that* boy?"

"Cal." Amberleigh smiled. "M'friend."

"What is the fascination with this boy?" His father's face was turning a dark shade of red. "He's a Boone. An apple never falls far from the tree and I—"

"He's a good kid, Dad." Brody shut him down. Cal couldn't pick who his family was. He sure as hell didn't want the boy judged for it. "His father, the *tree*, isn't part of his life and—"

"His grandfather doesn't have the time to teach him," his mother interrupted. "Can you imagine, Vic? My heart just breaks for the boy. All he wants is to ride in the cattle drive, but since he has no one to teach him, that's not going to happen now, is it?" She shook her head, making that face his father found impossible to resist. Brody knew. He'd seen her in action before. And her performances, while rare, were absolutely stunning. "So our son steps in and offers to help him. And you know what Cal said?" She sniffed, blinking rapidly. "He says, 'I can surprise my papa so he'll be proud of me.' Can you imagine?"

Brody stared. He'd told his mother an abridged version of the story, but to hear his mother tell it, she was right in the middle of it. And it was working. His father could be a cantankerous old coot, but he put his grandchildren first. As far as he was concerned, all men with grandchildren were obligated to do the same. His mother was using his father's weakness *and* playing the trump card—Woodrow Boone.

His father cleared his throat, instantly softening. "The boy said that?"

His parents both looked at him for confirmation. "He did," he agreed. It was the truth—even if his mother hadn't been the one to hear it.

His father's sigh was long and loud. "Where's the boy's father?" he asked, no longer bearing Cal any ill will.

"No daddy," Amberleigh said, shaking her head. "Cal. India. Tanner."

Brody stared at his daughter, stunned by the amount of words she'd just spoken. But Cal was important to his daughter. And, since they were talking about him, it made sense that she had something to add.

"No daddy?" his father repeated, clearing his throat again.

Brody caught his father's eye and shook his head, not wanting to share India's secret about her ex but needing his father to understand. It was better Cal's father wasn't in the picture.

His father's nod was stiff. "So he's left with his ma, a dog and a granddad who won't show him how to ride a horse."

Brody knew he had more than that. Cal was the sort of child who made friends wherever he went. And, even if Woodrow Boone was a pain in the ass, the rest of his family undoubtedly fawned over the boy.

"A dog that saved our granddaughters," his mother added. "Maybe even lost an eye doing it. Come help me get juice together for the girls, Vic."

Brody ran a hand over his face. She was up to something, but unless he wanted to call her on it, there wasn't much he could do about it. His parents left him with the girls.

"You two listen to Nana, okay?" he said. "If she says you're up for it, I'll stop and get you some ice cream on my way home. What kind?"

"Pink," Suellen said. "Please."

"I want brown and white." Marilyn smiled. "Or pink."

Brody laughed, running a hand over their foreheads. They'd had a few ear infections in the past. Their pediatrician had suggested tubes. He wasn't fond of the idea, but he sure hated seeing the girls laid up like this.

"Sorry," Amberleigh said, alternating pats between her sisters.

His parents emerged. His mother carried juice cups and a bottle of pain medicine for the girls. She wore a sympathetic smile, clucking and cooing as she gave them each a dose of sticky purple liquid to help fight their fever.

"Go?" Amberleigh asked, so excited she was practically bouncing.

"I'm ready." He nodded, glancing at his father. His father…wore an odd expression on his face. An expression Brody had never seen before.

"Vic." His mother nudged his father.

"What? Yes, all right, all right, Ramona." His father seemed to shake off whatever thoughts he'd been pondering so intently. "I'm going. Come on, Amberleigh. Let's get ready. You'll keep your boots on?"

Amberleigh nodded, sliding off her bed and running to her closet.

"I wanna go," Suellen cried.

"Me, too," Marilyn added, sniffing.

"We'll go again real soon," he promised, kissing their foreheads. "Right now you need to rest and feel better."

"You drink some juice and we'll watch the princess movie—with the swan. It's your favorite," his mother said. "You three go on. We'll be fine."

Brody scooped up Amberleigh and led his father from the girls' bedroom to the back door.

"It's a fine day for a ride," his father said, his eyes sweeping the clear blue sky.

"You know, you could check out Click's stock while we're there. We could use three, maybe four, new cutting horses." He shot his father a look, hoping there wouldn't be much resistance. Growing up, Brody's father hadn't been too keen on his friendship with Click Hale—the son of an abusive drunk who'd shocked the town with a murder-suicide scandal many locals were still shaken by. But over time Brody had tried to convince him Click was his own man, and a good one at that.

"Jared told me," his father said, climbing into Brody's truck. "He said Hale's doing good things—has only praises for his horses. Considering some of the ranches he's sold stock to, it seems he knows what he's doing. Guess I'll see for myself."

Which wasn't a *no*. Brody ran to the barn, dug out his old saddle and hurried back to his truck.

"Go, Daddy, go!" Amberleigh squealed as he started the vehicle. "See Cal."

He grinned. "We're on the way, sugar." There was no denying his excitement. It didn't matter he'd been with India just this morning—he was already missing her.

"You like the boy, so I'm assuming you like his mother, too?" his father asked, staring straight out the front windshield. "She's a pretty thing, no denying that. Shame she's a Boone."

Brody chuckled. "Her name might be Boone, but she's

her own person. I'm hoping you won't hold who her parents are against her."

His father glanced at him then. "You are? Well, I guess I'll see about that, too."

Chapter Fourteen

India followed Pearl and Banshee across the yard—after the chickens. For reasons her parents had yet to understand, Pearl liked to round up the chickens and herd them back into the chicken coop whenever she felt they'd wandered too far. Banshee, being an Anatolian shepherd, was obliged to help his favorite little human. The chickens, however, especially the rooster, didn't always appreciate the extra attention. It was India's job to make sure Pearl and the rooster didn't have a run-in.

"Petty," Pearl said, stooping to pick some tiny white flowers that had cropped up around the coop fence. "Petty," she repeated, holding them up to India.

"Those are pretty flowers, Pearl," she agreed.

Pearl nodded and rested the flower on Banshee's head, then clapped her hands in delight. India couldn't help but laugh, too.

The crunch of gravel under tires had them all turning to see Brody's bright red truck. He slowed, pulled off onto a patch of flattened grass and parked.

India's stomach was churning with all the best emotions. Happiness, want, pleasure and hope. How she'd let this happen, she didn't know. But it had. And now she watched Cal barrel toward the truck, waving his hat and smiling, with her heart in her throat. Watching Brody climb out, smiling one of his warmest smiles just for her boy, made her weak in the knees. He said something, making Cal laugh, before ruffling her son's shaggy hair. Her heart thumped hard against her rib cage.

But seeing Vic Wallace climb out of the passenger seat had an instant cooling effect. All the warm, sweet tingles froze with ice-cold dread.

"Let's go see who's here," India said, taking Pearl's hand. She let Pearl set the pace, the toddler still uncertain on her little legs—but determined all the same. Besides, Banshee wasn't about to let her fall. Tandy and Click beat them to the truck, shaking hands and making small talk as she and Pearl tottered their way.

"Mom," Cal called back. "Brody's here."

"I see that," she said when she reached the little group gathered around Brody's truck. "Good morning, Brody, Amberleigh and Mr. Wallace." Her smile grew when Amberleigh came running to her, arms outstretched for a hug. "How are you?" she asked, squatting and hugging the little girl close. "And where are your sweet sisters?"

"Bed. Sick." Amberleigh shrugged.

Tandy introduced the two girls to each other and led them back to the chicken coop with promises about holding one of the new chicks.

"I brought you something, Cal," Brody said, walking to the end of his truck to pull a large burlap lump from the truck bed.

"You didn't have to do that," India said, fully aware that Vic Wallace was studying her.

"A boy can't ride without a saddle," Mr. Wallace said.

"Besides, I outgrew it a few years back." Brody chuckled, pulling the burlap off the leather saddle. "You like it?"

Cal nodded, his eyes going round. "Do I ever."

India's heart was racing. Her son shone with happiness. And Brody... His gaze locked with hers just long enough to get her heart racing and her cheeks burning. What that man could do with one look wasn't fair.

She tore her gaze from his, hoping like hell her cheeks weren't giving her emotions away. A quick glance at Mr. Wallace told her she'd had no such luck. His tawny eyes, similar to his son's, were narrowed, his mouth pressed tight. He didn't look pleased...or displeased. *Surprised* was the best word. Surprised—with a good dose of shock.

"Nice to see you here this morning, Mr. Wallace," Click said.

Vic Wallace cleared his throat and tucked his thumbs into his belt loops. "Brody convinced me it might be worth my while. We need some ready-trained stock-friendly rides. Nothing that'll spook easy or that's too high-spirited."

Click nodded, his hands on his hips. "I've got a handful you can look at. I can get them saddled to ride if you'd like?"

India saw Brody open his mouth, then clap it shut. He might worry about what his father should or shouldn't do, but he knew better than to embarrass his father—especially in public. Pride was important to his father, and Brody understood that. And India loved the respect Brody gave his father.

Vic Wallace sighed, leveling a look at Brody. "My doc, and my boy, would have a fit if I rode today. But, if I like what I see, I'll ask you and Brody to put them through their paces?"

Click nodded. "Yes, sir. Why don't we go see what I've got. Come on, Cal, I'll show you Tommy. He's a mighty fine horse, just for you."

Cal did his best to carry the saddle but didn't argue

when Brody gripped the saddle cantle. His fingers wrapped around the thick rise at the saddle's rear, his forearm shifting beneath the weight, as he smiled down at Cal.

"You ready?" Brody asked.

"Yes, sir." Cal nodded, walking at Brody's side. "I could hardly sleep last night, thinking about today."

Brody glanced back at her. "I didn't get much sleep either, Cal. Maybe there was a full moon out."

She rolled her eyes and followed them to the barn, smiling. "I slept just fine. Like a baby," she sounded off, watching the muscle in Brody's jaw tick.

"I was worried about Tanner, too," Cal said. "Tandy says he'll be fine, but still. He always sleeps with me."

"He does?" Brody asked. "Not much room for you in the bed, then, huh?"

Cal giggled. "Nope."

"We'll get him as soon as your lesson's over, Cal," India said, catching up to ruffle his hair. "He'll be so happy to see you."

Cal nodded. "Me, too."

"Until then, you need to focus," Brody said, lifting the saddle and placing it on a saddle rack inside the barn. He stared down at Cal then, his tone growing serious. "Even on the best horse alive, a cowboy has to focus on riding. In time, it'll get to be second nature to you—like breathing. But, for now, I need you to promise you'll keep your ears open and your mind focused. Okay?"

Cal was listening intently. "Yes, sir. I promise."

Brody nodded. "I believe you're a man of your word, Cal."

And just like that Cal's posture stiffened and his chest swelled. Right before her eyes he went from little boy to a little man. "Always keep your word," she said. "People respect a man who keeps his word."

"Women, too?" Cal asked, glancing between them.

"Women, too." Brody winked at her.

"Cal," Click called from the other side of the barn. "Come over and see what you think of Tommy."

"Can I?" Cal asked her.

She nodded. "Listen to Click."

Cal was off, running down the row of stalls to where Click and Mr. Wallace stood, studying a pen full of horses.

"Can you grab that saddle pad?" Brody asked, nodding at the storage closet.

She stepped inside, eyeing the wall of saddle pads. Every size, shape and color hung on the wall. She turned back. "Which one—"

But Brody's arms slid around her waist and tugged her against him.

"What are you up to—?"

His lips were on hers, and she knew exactly what he was up to. She kissed him back with everything she had.

HE SHOULDN'T BE kissing her. Not with Cal and Click and his father so close. But he didn't seem to have a damn choice. Right now, having her in his arms was all that mattered. Now that he knew the sounds she made, the way she tasted and how passionate she was, he couldn't wait to have her alone.

"Brody," she whispered, her hands pressing against his chest. "Behave."

"You sure about that?" he asked, his mouth traveling down her neck to her throat.

Her breath hitched. "I'm sure… Your father…"

"Wouldn't blame me." But his hold eased.

She sighed, the smile on her face almost tempting him into another kiss. "Being charming again?"

He shook his head. "Honest. You're a beautiful woman, India Boone. Any man, my father included, would have to be blind not to see that."

"I'm pretty sure my looks have nothing to do with how your father feels about me." Her fingers slid through his hair. "Does Cal need a saddle pad or were you just trying to get me in here?"

Brody released her, his long-suffering sigh making her chuckle. "He needs one. But I've got it already."

She shook her head.

"You're saying you didn't want me to kiss you?" he asked.

She studied him, her arms wrapped around her waist. "I'm not saying that."

He grinned and walked out of the storage closet—and smack into his father's chest.

"Get lost?" his father asked.

"No, sir," he said, refusing to get flustered. "Just making sure we have everything we need to get Cal started."

"Now you do?" he asked, his gaze traveling beyond him.

"Now we do," he agreed, hefting the saddle onto his shoulder. "Any horses catch your eye?"

His father nodded, his gaze staying on India as she walked past them both and toward Cal. Brody pointedly ignored the look and followed her, supplies in tow.

"He's not too big." Cal was sizing up the compact dapple-gray quarter horse named Tommy.

"He's just the right size," Brody agreed. "Good temperament, too."

"So he's nice?" Cal asked.

"You think I'd let you get on a horse that wasn't?"

India asked, smiling bravely. She was trying her hardest to stay calm, but Brody could pick up on her nerves.

"Tommy's got some years on him," Click said. "He's got a sure step and a gentle spirit. I think you two will get on fine, Cal."

Brody let Click take the lead on the introductions, but he stayed close. Cal knew him best, and if he got panicked or needed more time, he wanted the boy to feel comfortable saying as much. He watched Cal with the horse, the way the horse sniffed him head to toe, and listened to Click's instruction on how to saddle a horse.

"I know how to do that," Cal said. "I've watched a million times. I've just never been allowed on a horse without my mom."

Brody smiled at India. Of course she would have ridden with him. She'd grown up in the saddle.

"You're old enough to ride on your own," Brody's father spoke up.

Brody tensed, but—much to his relief—India didn't. She nodded at his father.

Five minutes later everyone was out of the barn, and Cal was on horseback. Brody adjusted the stirrups, made sure the boy's helmet fit right and patted his leg. "You look good. You feel good?" he asked.

Cal nodded. "Yes, sir."

Brody watched the boy, proud of how carefully he listened to what he and Click and his father said. He was sharp as a tack. Tommy was a perfect fit, responsive to Cal without being jumpy or excitable. All in all, the boy's first lesson went far better than Brody could have hoped for.

"He's a natural," Mr. Wallace said as Cal and Tommy trotted past.

"Just look at that smile," India said, smiling herself.

"Cal ride?" Amberleigh asked, having joined them not too long ago.

"He is," India agreed, picking up his daughter. "Like a real cowboy. Just like your daddy and your grandpa."

Amberleigh nodded.

Brody did his best to hide the surge of love that swept over him. Here he was, his daughter, her son and the woman he loved most in the world. Cal's pride made him proud, too. India's sweet laugh, Amberleigh's giggle—hell, even his father's nod of approval at Cal's accomplishments—told him this was what he wanted. This was the life he was meant to have. The life Cal and his girls deserved.

"What's going on in that brain of yours?" his father whispered. "You've got that look on your face."

"What look?" he asked.

"That look you get when you're cooking something up." His father sighed. "Always thinking. Always wanting more. Life will be easier when you stop wanting, Brody."

He studied his father, pondering his words. He was right. Between the girls, being elected mayor and running all the family businesses, he should be happy. But now that he knew what could be, what should be, there was only one way he'd be truly happy.

Cal wanted to learn everything he could about taking care of Tommy. From brushing him down to cleaning his hooves to what he ate and why, the boy kept firing questions. Eventually India and Tandy rounded up the kids for some cookies and lemonade while he and his father went to look at horses again.

His father took his time, giving each animal a thorough once-over before nodding or shaking his head. Brody watched, making notes. His father had been running their ranch for a hell of a long time. One thing he'd learned from watching Cal today—take every opportunity to learn something new. When the horses were picked, they all headed inside for a snack.

"Lemonade?" Tandy asked. "Oatmeal raisin cookies?"

"Go get Tanner," Amberleigh said as soon as she'd taken a cookie.

"You're going to get Tanner?" Brody asked India.

"Just as soon as Cal's finished," India agreed.

"I wanted to thank you, Cal," his father spoke up, letting Amberleigh climb into his lap. "I hear your dog kept the girls from getting snake bit. I'm only sorry he wasn't as lucky."

Cal nodded. "He's a good dog, Mr. Wallace."

"Then you're a lucky boy," his father said.

Cal nodded again. "I think so."

"I had a dog when I was your age. She was big and mean to everyone but me and my mother. But she was like your Tanner, protecting me and going with me all over the place. She even chased off a black bear once— there were more of 'em around when I was a boy." His father sipped his lemonade, lost in the memories of his childhood.

"What was her name?" Cal asked, stretching his legs out in front of his chair like the rest of the men.

"Sally." His father nodded, taking a bite of the cookie. "Damn good dog."

Brody had grown up on stories about Sally. He'd never gotten a dog for fear it would never be able to match Sally. Then, somehow, he'd ended up with a lapdog.

"Sounds like it," Cal agreed.

"Tanner go?" Amberleigh asked.

"No, sugar, Tanner needs to go home with Cal and India. He's their dog. Like Lollipop is yours." Brody shook his head, watching his daughter rubbing her eyes.

She was worn out. Which meant she might just take a nap on the ride home.

"Who names a dog Lollipop?" his father grumbled. "He looks like a mop head, and his bark sounds like a chew toy."

The kitchen filled with laughter, India's included.

"Now, Dad, you can't blame the dog. He may not be much of a working dog, but he loves the girls all the same." He didn't know why he was defending the ball of fluff, but he was.

"And that's why I tolerate him," his father agreed. "Anything for my girls."

Brody saw wistfulness on India's face again. He didn't know Woodrow Boone personally. His father was convinced the man was the lowest sort of life form on the planet. But Brody held out hope that wasn't the case. He didn't know how or when, but Brody hoped there'd come a time when Woodrow Boone became the man his daughter and grandson needed him to be.

Chapter Fifteen

"You win again," India said, laughing. "Scarlett, you're up."

Scarlett had been watching their epic checkers showdown in growing dismay. Cal was a supercompetitive checkers player. Scarlett had made the mistake of saying she wanted to play the winner.

India normally did her best to avoid dinner at Fire Gorge, but this week had been nonstop, and getting a free dinner—with no cleanup—was too good an offer to pass up. Even if it was with her family at Fire Gorge ranch.

Tanner lay at Cal's feet, snoring softly. The dog had kept her and Cal smiling all week. He was so happy to be home, he didn't seem to mind that he'd lost his eye. Besides the occasional misjudged corner or step, it didn't seem to bother him. And any time he did stumble, he remembered the next time. Cal was on top of the world, showering his best friend with brushings and extra treats. Which was one of the reasons she'd need to go to the grocery store soon. But there'd been no time to shop this week.

After Cal's wonderful riding lesson, they'd picked up Tanner and headed home to four messages from teachers—which kept her week full. When she wasn't substitute teaching, she was at the shop poring over her textbooks and minding the store. And she'd managed to fit in a Monarch Festival committee meeting in her spare time—when all she really wanted was a nap.

When she fell into the bed at the end of each day, Brody's texts were waiting for her. From sweet to sexy, he made it clear he wanted to see her again—the sooner, the better. It was tempting. Her body was more than willing, aching in fact, but the reality was far more complicated.

Especially now that her heart was involved. How could it not be? She'd always known he was special. Even young, Brody Wallace had the ability to bring folks together and ease their worries. Watching her son enjoy both Brody's and Vic Wallace's company had almost made her believe there was a way for their families to come together.

"Tonight is the final installment of our special piece on Fort Kyle's soon-to-be-mayor, Brody Wallace. Join us for a visit to the Wallace ranch and meet the folks who helped make him the man he is today." Jan Ramirez smiled into the camera.

India stared at the television.

"Thank goodness that's almost over," her mother said. "In the paper and on the news, Brody Wallace is everywhere. And it's put your father in a foul temper."

India glanced at her sister. Scarlett rolled her eyes and went back to setting up the checkerboard.

"Mom?" Cal asked.

"What?" she asked, jostled from her thoughts.

"Gramma asked if you want tea or lemonade or water with dinner," Cal repeated.

"Oh, tea, please," she said, smiling up at her waiting mother.

"You all right, India?" her mother asked. "You seem worn out. I was wondering—"

"We were wondering," Scarlett said. "Why not let Cal spend the night with me tonight? We'd have fun, wouldn't we, Cal?"

Cal nodded. "Tanner, too?" Tanner lifted his head long enough for Cal to rub him behind the ear.

"Of course. Tanner, too," Scarlett agreed. "We can play checkers and you can show me that video game you like to play."

"It's a game app, Aunt Scarlett." Cal sighed.

Scarlett chuckled. "Fine. You can get the tablet and show me how to play that game with the knights and dragons."

All three of them looked her way, waiting for her answer.

"Dinner ready yet?" her father asked, stalking into the dining room. "I'm starving."

They followed him into the dining room, took their seats among the dude ranch's guests and began passing around platters of food. Fried chicken, corn on the cob, fluffy dinner rolls, macaroni and cheese and mashed potatoes with cream gravy. India took small helpings and loaded up on salad.

"That's all you're going to eat?" her mother asked. "You need to take care of yourself."

"Thanks, Mom, this is plenty." She smiled. Apparently mothers never outgrew worrying over what their kids ate.

"You're too skinny," her father said. "A man likes a little meat on a woman. About time you found a man for you and Cal, don't you think?"

"I do," Cal said. "I want a little brother or sister. So Mom has to get married first."

"She sure does." Her father nodded. "I wouldn't mind a few more grandkids."

"Woodrow," her mother interrupted. "Can you pass the pepper?"

The smile he shot her mother was full of real affection, prompting India to say, "I see the way you look at Mom, and I want that, too."

"Guess you learned something the first time around." Her father's brows rose. "If a man doesn't put you on a pedestal, he doesn't deserve you."

Her mother nodded. "But you can't afford to be too picky. Slim pickings here about."

"All too true." Her father nodded. Conversation shifted to the Monarch Festival and the various booths and committees, which led to the news. "They gave five minutes' time to promoting the festival, something that will bring in money to the town. But they find the time to sing Brody Wallace's praises all week. I'm not sure what this reporter's trying to prove—that he'll be a good mayor or that she's sweet on him."

"She was there when Tanner got bit." Cal served himself some macaroni. "They didn't act sweet on each other. And I'm real thankful Brody got Tanner to the vet clinic so fast. Tandy says he might not have made it if it wasn't for him." Cal promptly shoved a forkful of macaroni into his mouth.

India watched her parents closely. It was plain to see how much the Wallaces loved their grandchildren. But to see it on her parents' faces as they listened to Cal was a shock. Not her mother; she adored Cal. But her father... He was listening to every word Cal said. And it touched her heart to know her boy mattered to him. Even if it took a dangerous snake incident for her dad to show it.

"He carried Tanner, and Mom and that lady carried his girls, and we all ran to his truck," Cal said, shaking his head. "I was so scared, but he was real nice to me."

"Nice to know the boy doesn't take after his father," her father said. "Maybe his time away from home took some of the Wallace starch out of him."

India didn't say a word, hoping conversation would move into more neutral territory. Eventually it did. Possible changes to the dude ranch's long-standing theme nights, Cal's schoolwork and her mother's regular plea for a vacation filled the rest of the meal. Her mother had been trying to tempt her father into a romantic getaway since India could remember.

"Your anniversary is coming up. Maybe, this year, you could go somewhere, Dad?" Scarlett suggested, smiling sweetly.

"It's not a good time to be leaving Fire Gorge," he said, avoiding eye contact with everyone around the table.

"It's never a good time." Their mother sighed. "Maybe we should go, girls. A mother-daughter trip." This was the first time their mother had suggested going somewhere without their father.

And the look of surprise on her father's face was priceless.

By the time dessert was cleared away and Scarlett and Cal had returned to their checkers game in the den, India was wiped out. She was just about to doze off in the recliner opposite her father when he woke her. "See what I mean?" He pointed at the television.

Brody was there, walking along the fort, smiling—looking charming and sweet and warm. She knew just how warm he could be. How strong and giving he was. He would give all to this town, to his daughters and the woman he picked to spend the rest of his life with.

"Damn shame he's a Wallace. If he wasn't, I might actually like the boy." Her father's words were soft.

She wanted to defend Brody—to tell her father all the reasons his last name shouldn't matter.

"When is your truck going to be ready?" he asked, out of the blue.

"In a week."

Daniel wasn't in any hurry, but he was charging half what the garage wanted, so she'd wait for him.

"Good." Her father glanced at her, the ghost of a smile on his face—then it was gone. "Good." There were times she could almost convince herself that he respected her and truly cared for her. Almost. But if that were true, he wouldn't have turned her away when she needed him most, wouldn't look at her like he did most days.

She nodded and pushed out of the recliner, said her goodbyes and walked the path to her cabin—eager to put some distance between her and her father.

When Brody's text rolled in, she stared at it for a long time.

Missing you.

Brody knocked on the cabin door, his heart in his throat.

He'd spent the better part of the week missing India, aching for her, and he'd let her know in his texts. Yet she hadn't made time to see him all week. Tonight, she finally had.

I'm alone. Come if you can.

Was that really all he was to her? A hookup? Someone to see when she was alone?

Still, he was the one who had said he'd take whatever she gave him. If she wanted him, he was powerless to resist. He'd made sure the girls were sleeping, then paused in the living room. His father was sound asleep in his recliner, and his mother was knitting. She hadn't batted an eye when he told her he was going out.

Now he stood in the dark, knocking on the door, feeling like a damn fool.

He knocked again, more firmly this time, and slipped inside. "India?"

Nothing. No light, no sound, no sign of India. Only a faint light spilling out from under her bedroom door. Which irritated him all the more.

But once he'd pushed the door wide, he paused, his irritation gone. She was sound asleep, her hair spilling over her pillow and her arm resting atop the sheet and quilt that covered her.

He was torn. He wanted to stay, badly, but he didn't want to wake her up. With all the sickness and germs he'd been battling this week, he had a whole new respect for the restorative powers of sleep. All three girls and his mother had ended up on antibiotics, but they were all, thankfully, on the mend.

Besides, he was tired. And nothing sounded better than sleeping. With India.

He kicked off his boots and climbed onto the bed beside her.

"Brody?" she whispered, her hand sliding up his arm to tug on his sleeve. "You're dressed. Off."

He chuckled but did as she said, then slid beneath the sheets in his boxers. "I feel bad for waking you."

She rolled over him, naked and warm from sleep. "I wanted you to wake me up."

His lungs emptied as he stared up at her. "I'll never get tired of looking at you," he whispered, his hands sliding up her sides, relishing each shudder his touch elicited.

She smiled, leaning into the brush of his fingers

against her breasts. "You're still overdressed." Her fingers slid along the waist of his boxer shorts.

"I thought we were sleeping." His hands cradled her breasts, savoring the weight and feel in his palms.

"We will," she moaned, arching.

He sat up, sucking the tip of one breast into his mouth. His teeth and tongue worked it over, relentless, until the peak grew pebble-hard. His mouth trailed from beneath the swell of her breast, along her side and back up again—loving the other breast until her fingers bit into his scalp and her breath powered from her in heavy bursts.

"I missed you." He slid his hands into her hair, holding her still until her gaze met his. "I looked for you all week, hoping to see you smile."

"Your texts were the last thing I saw before I went to bed." Her gaze was heavy—with more than wanting. "They made me smile. You make me smile."

He kissed her, once, so soft it was a whisper. "Stay, India. Don't leave." He held her when she would have pulled away, deepening the kiss until she was clinging to him again. He rolled over her, discarding his boxers, before she flipped them again.

She was now on top, and her heat enveloped him, ripping a groan from his chest. His hands clasped her hips, holding her still, holding her tightly against him. She looked incredible. Breathing hard, hair mussed and eyes glazed with hunger—for him. He could stay like this for hours.

But she began to move.

He'd introduced her to passion. Now she was relentless, straining against him, arching her hips, resting her hands on his thighs, giving it her all. He fought his own desire, determined to see her fall apart before his climax reached him. He thrust up, seating himself so deep it jolted him to his core. Over and over she joined them together until she was trembling. He felt her response, the tiny quivers and spasms that spread through her, until she was crying out his name.

He smiled, rolling over her and driving into her. His body came alive for her, craved her, needed her. And so did his heart. He loved her, loved loving her.

Her head fell back, her body clenching again as he welcomed the power of his release.

He collapsed at her side, heart racing and breathing hard. She rested her cheek against his chest, the beat of her heart racing against his side. It would be all too easy to get used to this. Nothing compared to having India Boone in his arms, nothing. He wanted her at his side for the rest of his days, as his wife, raising their children together, maybe adding some more along the way.

He'd spent too much time thinking about the future she didn't want. And now, instead of enjoying the here and now, all he could think about was what he was losing. "Would you think about giving us a real chance?" he asked, his voice gruff. "For me?"

She stared up at him, cheeks flushed, breathing heavy, and so surprised he cursed himself. He didn't want to lose this. Even though he wanted to believe they were growing closer, she might not feel the same.

"What does that mean? For you?" Her voice was soft and thready.

He ran a hand along her cheek. "Last weekend here, and our time with the kids, felt good—like the start of something real. Let's give this a chance to see where it could go—no secrets, no letting our families dictate our choices…and you being open-minded about staying in Fort Kyle." His gaze searched hers.

She stared at him, flashes of a dozen thoughts and feelings rushing across her face. "We agreed, Brody…" She swallowed, her explanations stalling out. "What I needed, what I thought we both needed, hasn't changed. Has it?"

The sincerity of her voice plucked at his heart. Nothing had changed for him. He loved her. And he was a fool for thinking he could make her love him. "What did you need, India?"

She frowned. "I needed *you*. The way you make me feel when you're around. Just…you. I didn't mean to upset you."

"You didn't upset me. You've told me from the beginning how things stand." He shook his head. "I thought I could be fine with just this—"

"Just this?" She frowned. "This *is* something."

But not enough. He had a choice to make. Tell her the truth and stop this from ever happening again or accept the way things were. He was the one who was making this hard, not her. It wasn't fair to get upset now, simply because she hadn't come around to his way of thinking. But, maybe, it wasn't fair to his heart to let things go on.

"It is," he agreed, his hand cradling her cheek. He might regret it, but there were things that needed to be said. "Enough to make me want more."

She stared at him, so still and quiet he didn't know what to make of it.

He kissed her. "When I'm with you I have the future I want. Right here. You, me, Cal, the girls, in Fort Kyle."

"Brody, stop." Tears spilled down her cheeks, but still she didn't move.

"I know our families will take their own sweet time coming around, but they will—"

"No, they wouldn't. My father would never come around, Brody. He'd be mean and hateful to you—and that would put Cal in the middle. And your girls, too."

She shook her head. "And your family? I won't drive a wedge between you and your family."

"There's no way of knowing how things would turn out," he argued.

"None," she agreed. "We both know that. Neither of our first marriages had this kind of baggage going in. We're lonely and being a single parent is hard, but that's real life. It doesn't matter how much I love you or if you love me, it won't suddenly fix everything—that's *not* real life. I'd rather spare our kids than risk their happiness."

He stared at her, filtering through her words. She loved him. She might not have realized she'd said it, but he sure as hell did. She loved him, but it wasn't enough. "So where does that leave us?"

She drew in a deep breath, bracing herself. "Nothing's changed, Brody. This is all I can give you. If you still want it."

He smiled, burying the hurt deep down inside him. "When it comes to you, I'll take whatever I can get, India Boone." He kissed her gently, ignoring the pain as she slipped her arms around him and held him close.

Chapter Sixteen

India's phone started ringing a little after five in the morning.

"Is that you or me?" Brody asked, reaching over her to turn on the bedside lamp.

"Me." She took the phone he offered, instantly recognizing Scarlett's number. "Scarlett?"

"Cal's not feeling well," Scarlett said. "His throat's hurting him and he wants to come home."

"Of course," she said. "I'll walk up and get him."

"No, Dad's got him—"

"Dad?" She bolted from the bed. "Are they... Is he coming out here? To my cabin?"

"Cal was crying." Scarlett broke off. "Oh my God, is Brody there? I'll try to stop him. Dammit, I'm so sorry, India. I'll try to stall him a bit."

"My dad's coming," she said, tossing the phone onto the bed and throwing clothing at Brody. "Now."

"Is Cal okay?" Brody asked, tugging on his jeans.

"Sore throat," she said, tugging on her plain white cotton nightgown. "Why aren't you moving faster?"

"That's pretty." He nodded at her nightgown. "Girls had it. Get him on antibiotics. He'll feel better in a couple of days—"

"Brody," she interrupted, pushing him toward the

door. "You can't be here. My dad... Cal... You have to go. Now."

To her surprise, he smiled. "I'm going, India." He shook his head. "If Cal's up for it, we'll go ahead with our next riding lesson at Click's Sunday."

She opened the door, pushing his broad back with both hands. "I'll tell him. Go."

He climbed into his truck wearing his boots and jeans, tossed his shirt in the passenger seat and started the engine.

India held her breath, watching as his taillights disappeared—as Cal and her father appeared on the trail leading to her front door. Tanner loped ahead, pressing his head against her thigh before trotting back to Cal.

"Mom," Cal said, wiping his nose with the back of his hand. "I'm sick."

She stooped, pressing a hand to his forehead.

"He's got a fever, but your ma already gave him some medicine," her father said, an undeniable edge to his voice.

"The pink stuff that tastes like bubble gum," Cal said, letting her pick him up. Which told her just how bad he must feel.

"I appreciate that, Dad." She smiled at him. "I would have walked up to get him."

"Already up," her father said, following her inside and sitting on her lumpy couch.

India lingered, thankful she and Brody had confined their escapades to her room. Still, she scanned the room, nervous he'd find something. "Want something to drink?" she asked. "I can make you some coffee after I put Cal to bed."

"Take your time," he said, his voice low and steady. He was clipped and measured—like he was fighting for control. It made her anxious. But her father could wait until Cal was settled. "Okay," she said, carrying Cal into his room. "Want some water?" she asked her son.

He nodded. "And Tanner," he said, patting his bed. "Come on, boy."

Tanner jumped up and rested his massive head on the pillow beside Cal.

"He can't catch it, can he?" Cal asked, running his hand along the dog's side.

"No, I'm pretty sure he's safe," she said, turning off the overhead and clicking on his night-light. "I'll be right back with your water."

Her father watched her get Cal a drink. "Want something?" she asked.

He shook his head. "Take your time."

She hurried back into Cal's room. "Need anything else?" Balancing on the edge of the bed was no easy feat. Between Cal and Tanner, there wasn't much room for her. She smoothed the hair from her son's forehead with her other hand. "Sorry you feel bad."

He shook his head, his eyes already closed. "I wanted to come home."

"Well, you are," she assured him, pressing a kiss against his overheated skin. "Sleep tight, baby. I'm right next door if you need anything. We'll go to the doctor first thing."

"'Kay, Mom, I love you." He rolled over, threw an arm over Tanner and yawned.

India stayed where she was, watching his breathing steady and slow in sleep. Tanner's soft snore filled the still room. She smiled, patted Tanner on the side and left, leaving the door partially cracked.

"You okay, Dad?" she asked, wanting to get this over with.

He nodded. "I'd planned on coming over here to make peace. You know, tell you how damn proud I am of you for working so hard and doing such a good job with Cal. And you are—he's a good boy."

She was dreaming. Surely. "Thank you," she managed, even though it sounded more like a question.

"But then I see something that tells me my feelings still don't matter to you." He pushed off the couch. "Brody Wallace?" He cleared his throat. "What did I do to make you hate me, India?"

"I don't hate you." She was in shock. "Dad, I've never hated you."

"You certainly don't like me. That much is clear. You have that man here, on my property—property his father accuses me of stealing." He shook his head. "It seems to me your choice in men hasn't improved with time. And, like last time, you're picking the person I like the least."

She couldn't decide which was greater—her anger or her incredulity. Did he really believe she'd picked Brody just to get to him? Or that Brody and JT could be lumped into the same category? Yes, they were both men. But, as far as India could tell, that was the only thing they had in common. JT was an embarrassment to mankind. Brody a shining example of what a man should be.

"Was it because I wouldn't come get you when your marriage started to fall apart?" her father asked, sincerely puzzled. "You still hold that against me?"

"You're asking?" she asked.

"I thought I just did."

She drew in a steadying breath. If he was asking, she would answer him. Even if it was hard for both of them to hear. "Hold it against you? No, Dad. Does it still hurt? Yes. I didn't want to call you. I knew how you felt about JT, I knew you hadn't forgiven me for marrying him.

But…I was scared and I needed help. So I called, hoping you'd help me—angry or not." His dismissive refusal had been salt in the wound, but she'd refused to beg.

"Scared?" he asked, frowning. "I've never done a thing to make you afraid of me, India."

"Not you, Dad." She avoided his gaze then. "JT. I was afraid of JT. You were right. He was a bad man. But you made me figure it out on my own, helped me grow stronger—for me and Cal. I needed that."

The silence grew heavy and thick, pressing in on her until she had no choice but to look at him. There were tears in his eyes. Her big, loud, opinionated father was crying for the first time in her life. "What are you saying?" The question was a whisper, raw and broken and anguished.

"Nothing that matters now," she mumbled.

But her father continued to stare at her until she was crying, too.

"I didn't know, India. How could I have known?" he asked.

She shook her head, wiping the tears from her face. "How could I tell you? I was ashamed by what he did to me. I couldn't listen to how, somehow, it was my fault. It was hard enough without hearing that from you."

"Oh, India." He hugged her awkwardly. "No, no, baby girl. No." He sniffed, his arms shaking around her. "I called you two days later, so mad at the things I'd said. But your phone was disconnected. I thought you were shutting us out—"

"No, Dad, Cal and I were…getting away."

"That *bastard* never deserved you. No man should lay a hand on you. Not ever, you hear me? It's not your fault. No, ma'am." His voice broke. "I should have… I should have… Your mother says I never shut the hell up and listen. She's right. Dammit all, she's right. India, I'm sorry. I'm so sorry."

She held on to her father then, needing his arms around her.

"You've never embarrassed or shamed me, India. Never. I was hurt and acted like a damn fool. You were so determined to leave home, so determined to do it on your own. You didn't want or need me, and I didn't know how to stand by and do nothing." He shook his head. "I let my temper get a hold of me. But I swear to you, it won't happen again. I'm old, I'm loud and I'm damn opinionated. But you're my baby girl, and I will always love you. Even when I'm being an ass. I'm sorry you ever doubted that."

She stared up at her father through her tears, the cracks in her heart shrinking.

"We'll talk tomorrow," he said, pressing a kiss to her temple. "I'm too beat to talk more. But, I'm sorry for not being there when you needed me. I'm sorry for being so damn pigheaded and selfish, sometimes." He stepped back, wiping a hand across his face. "But we will talk about the Wallace boy, you hear me?"

She nodded.

"Good," he said, heading toward the door. "Now, you get some sleep while Cal's resting and I'll see you later on."

She nodded again, words sticking in her throat and making it hard to breathe.

"I love you India. I do." He smiled. "Like any father, I only want the best for you. And your boy."

DAMMIT ALL, HE'D made eye contact with Woodrow Boone—eye contact. And he didn't know what to do about it. If he turned around and went back, he'd be doing what India didn't want—putting Cal in the middle. But driving away, leaving her to deal with her father's fallout alone, didn't sit well with him.

He pulled off the dirt road, waited ten minutes, then looped around to park in front of her little cabin. He wasn't sure what he'd expected, but finding her sobbing, alone, on her old lumpy couch wasn't it. His heart broke for her. "What can I do?" he asked, sitting at her side and pulling her in his arms.

"This," she said, burying her face against his throat.

"You want to talk about it?" he asked. "I'll listen."

But she was crying too hard to manage a word. He held her, mumbling nonsense and running his hand down her back until she relaxed against him. When her tears dried up, the words started. He didn't want to hear any of it, but it all came out. Her father's desertion and JT's abuse. That she'd faced it all alone, bouncing between friends from couch to couch, and that she'd spent nights in her truck along the way. Her pride had kept her from returning to Fort Kyle until she'd had no choice.

"He apologized," she finished, her voice rough. "Now, when I'd come to terms with the fact that he never would. Now, when I'd accepted I was alone."

"You were never alone," he ground out. "I would have come running."

"I did think about it." Her voice was soft and thick. "But so much time had passed and we'd gone our separate ways without Fort Kyle to keep us together. But I should have known you'll always be there for me, Brody, even when I try to push you away."

He closed his eyes, swallowing back all the things he wanted to say to her. Then he gave up. "I know why you push me away."

"You do?" Her blue-green eyes locked with his.

"You think letting someone in makes you weaker." He kissed her forehead. "But I've got news for you, India Boone. Whether you let me or not, I already love you. I've loved you since before I can remember, and I always will."

The flare of panic in her gaze gave way to tenderness. No, dammit, there was love there—he saw it, knew it and welcomed it with open arms. She could fight all she wanted, her heart had already decided. She loved him. And knowing that had him smiling like a damn fool.

Her hand pressed against his cheek.

He sighed, pressed a kiss against her palm and stared out the small window. Pink and yellow rays peaked over the horizon, signaling the arrival of dawn. He was running out of time—and there was something he needed to do before he could go home to his girls. "I need to get home before the girls realize I'm gone."

She blinked. "Now?"

"Want me to stay?" he asked.

"No. Yes." She slid from his lap and stood, looking at him.

"You don't have to know anything. Not yet. For now, put your worries aside and rest." He squeezed her hands, letting her fingers slide from his, as he made his way to her door. He paused then, smiling at her. "Everything is going to be okay, you know that?"

She stiffened, nodding. "Yes."

That was what she did, acted tough—to prove she didn't need anyone. Even when she did.

"Good." He winked and headed outside. It was a good morning, crisp and full of promise. He drove down the dirt road to the main house, parked and cursed himself for a damn fool. If he had to beg Woodrow Boone, he would. Since he didn't have time to shower and clean up, he shook the wrinkles from his shirt, tucked himself in and adjusted his belt. There wasn't much he could do about the stubble on his jaw, but he was otherwise presentable.

What he had to say to Woodrow Boone wouldn't take long, but he didn't want to wait.

The main lodge was waking up, servers setting the table with fresh linens and the slight kitchen noises that promised a big breakfast buffet for the dude ranch's guests.

"Brody Wallace?" Mrs. Boone saw him first. "What are you doing here?"

"I came to see your husband, Mrs. Boone. I know it's early, but I was hoping he'd be up." Somehow, he doubted Woodrow had come back from India's place and gone to bed. Likely he was all fired up and agitated over what she'd told him.

She glanced around, growing nervous. "May I ask why you're here? Now? Before he's had his coffee." Her smile grew tight as her husband walked into the room, Scarlett close behind.

"Good morning," he said. "Scarlett."

"Hi, Brody," she stammered, glancing from her father to him and back again. "You're here bright and early."

Woodrow Boone shook his head. "Why?"

He cleared his throat. "I've come to ask permission to marry your daughter." He held up a hand. "Before you tell me all the reasons why I can't marry her, I'd like to share the reasons I should."

"Why the hell would I listen to a thing you have to say?" Woodrow growled.

"Woodrow," his wife gushed. "Calm down. He's being nothing but polite."

"Daddy, hear him out, please," Scarlett said.

"And, for crying out loud, do not cause a scene in front of the guests," his wife pleaded.

Not that anyone was suggesting they move to a less crowded room to carry on the conversation. Which meant Mrs. Boone and Scarlett might just be on his side. He sure as hell hoped so. He had to give it to Woodrow. The man's jaw muscle was clenched tight, his nostrils flared, but he nodded.

"I love her. I've loved her since she brought an arrowhead to show-and-tell in Mrs. Carmichael's kindergarten class. She used to love those things, like Cal. And I love that boy. I'll never treat her, her son or your family with anything but respect. I believe in family, Mr. and Mrs. Boone. And, if India and Cal agree to be my family, that would mean we're all family." He cleared his throat. "Also, I'll do whatever I can to make them both happy, here in Fort Kyle."

That made Woodrow pause. He saw it. He wanted India to stay almost as much as he did. "And if she wants to go?" Woodrow Boone forced the words out.

"If she wants to go, we'll go. Together." He meant it. "But I think you fixed most of the reasons she had for leaving, Mr. Boone."

"Why? Woodrow, what did you do? What happened?" Mrs. Boone asked, glancing back and forth between them.

Brody didn't say a word. He wasn't about to deprive the man of his moment. And, he could tell, Scarlett and Mrs. Boone were going to be impressed. "I apologized to our girl. Something I should have done years ago." Woodrow Boone was studying him. "Told her she deserved only the best."

"Oh, Woodrow," his wife said, hugging her husband. "Thank you."

Woodrow's arm settled around his wife's shoulder, but his gaze stayed pinned on Brody. "You know I don't approve of you."

"I do." Brody nodded. "And I know I don't deserve her."

"But you think marrying you will keep her here? And happy?" Woodrow Boone asked. "You have an awfully high opinion of yourself, don't you?"

"No, sir," he said. "But, I give you my word, no man will work as hard as I will, every day, to make sure she and Cal know I love them." He swallowed. "I just need your blessing."

"She wants to marry you?" he asked.

"She loves me, I know that. But I haven't asked her," Brody confessed. "I wouldn't do that until I'd spoken with you."

"What about your father?" Mr. Boone asked.

"He likes her. He likes Cal. So does my mother." He saw no point in beating around the bush. "It's hard not to."

Mrs. Boone looked on the verge of tears. "You really do love her, don't you?"

"I do," he said.

"And if I say no?" Woodrow asked, ignoring his wife's gasp and Scarlett's whispered, "Daddy."

"I'll accept it, for today." He smiled. "And I'll be back, every morning for coffee, until you change your mind."

For the first time in Brody Wallace's life he saw something he never thought he'd see in Woodrow Boone's eyes. It looked a hell of a lot like respect.

Chapter Seventeen

The morning of the Monarch Festival was bright and crisp. After sneaking in a riding lesson every chance they got, Cal was ready to ride. Brody and Click were confident her boy would have a grand time riding in today's cattle drive. And, to make certain, they'd offered to ride with him—even though it was a traditional Boone event.

"You sure you're ready?" India asked Cal, for the hundredth time.

"I'm sure." Cal nodded, dressed in his parade finery, complete with chaps and a new hat.

"You sure look like a cowboy." She tapped the rim of his hat.

"I can ride like one, too." He grinned up at her.

"All right," she said, leading him out to the corrals. She caught sight of her father on the far side of the holding pen. Men of all ages milled about, laughing and joking in the cool morning air.

Click waved Cal over, Tommy already saddled and ready for the short ride through town.

"Gotta go, Mom," he said, running toward Click.

And Brody. Her heart turned over at the wink he sent her way. The last few weeks had been different. He didn't hide the way he felt about her anymore—instead he went out of his way to show her just how special she was to him.

Stolen kisses. Holding hands. Flowers. Notes and texts. But he hadn't visited her bed.

He wanted to. She could tell when their kisses lasted too long or his hold grew a little too impatient. Every time he'd back off. And it was driving her out of her mind. She ached for him. Missed him.

And loved him.

If he said it again, she might just come clean. She was tempted—more than tempted. But loving him didn't change the way their families felt about each other. Or the drama their children would have to endure if they did try for something more.

Cal's wave drew her back to the present. He sat atop Tommy, smiling for all the world to see. Her father included.

She held her breath as her father nudged his horse across the corral to Cal, Brody and Click. It was too far away to hear what was being said, but none of them looked tense or upset. Nope, there were smiles all around.

Her father was proud.

Cal was prouder.

"You ready to go?" Scarlett asked. "Looks like the menfolk have things under control here." She laughed.

They drove into town to set up the booths for the festival. Once the cattle crossed Main Street, the festival officially began. There'd be funnel cake and lemonade, bobbing for apples, Old West reenactments, face painting and butterfly-themed arts and crafts galore.

She set up the Butterfly Kissing Booth. Her two hours were early, so that should cut down on any too-drunk festivalgoers hoping for a real kiss, but still… She didn't like the idea of kissing unless it included Brody.

As the committee members finished their work, hundreds of thousands of monarch butterflies flew overhead. India stopped to stare up at them.

"Wow," she said.

"India." Amberleigh's voice reached her seconds before the little girl was at her side. "Look," she said, pointing up at the cloud of butterflies.

"Aren't they beautiful?" India asked, kneeling beside her.

"Pretty," Suellen said, her eyes wide and her little hands clasped together.

"Lots and lots," Marilyn added, spinning.

"You need butterfly crowns," India said. "All fairy princesses at the butterfly festival need crowns."

"They sure do," Ramona Wallace said, slightly out of breath from running after the girls. "Nice to see you, India."

"You, too," she said. "Come to help make crowns?"

"Of course." The woman nodded. "What colors?"

India didn't mind the glue or glitter coating her fingertips and hands when it was all said and done. The girls were laughing, winding pipe cleaners with feathers, paper butterflies and leaves, and adding ribbons and streamers.

Marilyn's was pink, Suellen's was blue and Amberleigh's was green—with just enough orange to show off the butterflies.

"You and Nana," Amberleigh said, setting to work.

"She's getting so good with her words," Mrs. Wallace said. "Guess she finally decided she had something to say."

India smiled, letting the girls make her an over-the-top crown with every color butterfly imaginable. And extra glitter.

"My," Mrs. Wallace said, her eyes round. "Don't you look sparkly?"

India laughed. "Make sure you put extra glitter on Nana's."

"Mind if we join you?" India's mother asked, sitting opposite Mrs. Wallace. "Nice to see you, Ramona."

"Good morning, Evelyn," Mrs. Wallace said, smiling. "Looks like a perfect day for a festival."

"Doesn't it, though?" her mother agreed.

India shot a look at her sister, but Scarlett just shrugged. "You've got crowns, now we need to make wings. So you can fly."

The girls' wings were done when the first cows appeared at the head of Main Street.

"Fly this way, girls," India said. "Watch and see. I bet you'll see some people you know riding this way."

The girls flapped their arms, their fabric wings and colorful ribbons blowing in the morning breeze. They lit up when they saw Cal, waving and calling his name. Good boy that he was, he nodded, keeping the reins in both hands. He sat tall in the saddle, Brody on one side, Click on the other. And her father bringing up the rear.

"Daddy!" Amberleigh called, so delighted the other two clapped and squealed, too.

"He's so handsome," her sister whispered.

"He is," she agreed, unable to take her eyes off Brody.

He waved at his girls and blew kisses, his tawny eyes crinkling and full of love. He loved her, too. He'd said so. And, according to Brody, a man's word was his promise.

"India?" her mother nudged her. "You okay?"

She nodded, unable to explain how right everything was in the moment. "I'm happy, Mom."

Her mother and sister hugged her tight. Life couldn't get much better.

BRODY SPOTTED HIS girls before they saw him. All of his girls, India, too.

They were working the Butterfly Kissing Booth, his girls laughing every time India had to brush her eyelashes across someone's cheek. Brody was glad they were butterfly kisses. The idea of India kissing another man, even for charity's sake, didn't sit well.

"What's Mom wearing?" Cal asked.

"Looks like a butterfly crown." Brody smiled. She looked beautiful. And shiny.

"Girls are weird." Cal sighed.

"They are," he agreed. "Good thing we love 'em."

Cal nodded, patting Tanner. "She's a good mom. You'll be real lucky if she says yes."

"I will," Brody agreed, his own butterflies churning in his stomach. When he'd imagined this, it had seemed easy—and romantic. Now, he wasn't so sure.

"Daddy." Suellen waved. "Butterfly kisses."

"I'll take one from you," he said, leaning forward to accept a butterfly kiss from his daughter. "Now a real one."

Suellen kissed him hard, wrapping her arms around his neck and holding on. "Love you, Daddy."

"Love you, too." He smiled at Marilyn. "I want one from you."

Marilyn was shy, quickly batting her lashes against his cheek and leaning away.

"No kiss?" he asked, offering her his cheek.

She smiled and kissed him.

"Thank you, Marilyn." He looked at Amberleigh. Marilyn and Suellen had fanciful face paint—making their butterfly ensemble complete. But Amberleigh's face was painted like a dragon. It made him chuckle. "You giving out dragon kisses?" he asked.

She shook her head. "Dino-roar," she said, smiling at Cal.

"I'll take one of those," Brody said. "As long as it won't hurt."

India laughed then.

"Careful," Amberleigh said, kissing him on each cheek. "There."

"I like dino-roar kisses." He looked at India then. "But I might have saved the best for last."

India's cheeks turned a lovely shade of pink. "Brody," she warned, glancing around them. She'd softened toward him over the past few weeks but was still skittish about anything public, knowing the feud, the election and the kids still complicated things.

"One butterfly kiss from you, Miss Boone," he said, putting his dollar in the jar, leaning forward and offering her his cheek.

She hesitated before brushing her extralong lashes across the ridge of his cheek a good half a dozen times.

"That was some kiss," he said, smiling down at her. "I like your crown."

"We made it," Suellen said.

"You've got glitter...all over," he said, running his fingers along India's cheek.

Her eyes went round. "Brody." She stepped back, her cheeks on fire then.

"I think I'm going to buy another kiss," he said, pulling the envelope from his back pocket and sliding it into the jar.

India frowned, pulling the envelope out. "What are you up to?"

He grinned. "Open it and find out."

"Yea, Mom." Cal was grinning, too, his excitement barely contained.

She opened the letter and read the paper inside. Once, then again. "It's a deed." She frowned. "To… What is it?"

"Our property, you know, the one the Wallaces and Boones have been squabbling over for the last few decades?" He grinned. "A place for our family. A wedding present from your father and mine. And a truce. As long as you say yes."

The paper fluttered out of her fingers.

He knelt, fully aware that a crowd had gathered around them and not caring a bit. "India Boone—"

"No, Brody, get up." She grabbed his hand and tugged frantically.

"Let the boy be," her father said. "You have no idea how determined he is."

"Don't I know it," Vic Wallace said. "He gets it from his mother."

Ramona Wallace shook her head.

India glanced at her father, then at Brody's, her green-blue eyes wide when they returned to him.

He took her hand in his. "You didn't think I'd let a little family feud stop me from marrying the woman I love."

She blinked, eyes sparkling. "I love you, too."

His heart thumped against his ribs, so damn full it was hard to breathe. "Then marry me, India. Make me the happiest man in Texas." He shook his head. "Whatever you want, wherever we go, we go together."

She stared at him, the sweet smile on her face enough for him. But, not, apparently, for Cal.

"Hurry up and answer him, Mom. I want a little brother or sister, remember?" And, just like that, every person in Fort Kyle was laughing.

Brody stood and tugged her into his arms. "Still thinking? I mean it, we don't have to stay—"

"This is home, Brody. Where I want to raise our family. Where I want to grow old with you." She cradled his face in her hands.

"I'll take that as a *yes*." He kissed her, a whisper of a kiss.

"Yes, it's a *yes*." She kissed him. "I love you, Brody Wallace. I always will."

"And she's a woman of her word," Cal said.

"I'll hold you to it, India." He smiled. "Every damn day for the rest of my life."

* * * * *

MILLS & BOON

Coming next month

MISS WHITE AND THE SEVENTH HEIR
Jennifer Faye

Of all the bedrooms, why did she have to pick that one?

Trey frowned as he struggled to get all five suitcases up the stairs. The woman really needed to learn how to pack lighter.

At the top of the steps, he paused. It was a good thing he exercised daily. He rolled the cases back down the hallway to the very familiar bedroom. The door was still ajar.

"Sage, it's just me." He would have knocked but his hands were full trying to keep a hold on all of the luggage.

There was no response. Maybe she'd decided to explore the rest of the house. Or perhaps she was standing out on the balcony. It was one of his favorite spots to clear his head.

But two steps into the room, he stopped.

There was Sage stretched across his bed. Her long dark hair was splayed across the comforter. He knew he shouldn't stare, but he couldn't help himself. She was so beautiful. And the look on her face as she was sleeping was one of utter peace. It was a look he'd never noticed during her wakeful hours. If you knew her, you could see something was always weighing on her mind. And he'd hazard a guess that it went much deeper than the trouble with the magazine.

Though he hated to admit it, he was impressed with the new format that she'd rolled out for the magazine. But he wasn't ready to back down on his campaign to close the magazine's doors. None of it changed the fact that to hurt his father in the same manner that he'd hurt him, the magazine had to go. It had been his objective for so many years. He never thought he'd be in a position to make it happen—but now as the new CEO of QTR International, he was in the perfect position to make his father understand in some small way the pain his absence had inflicted on him.

Trey's thoughts returned to the gorgeous woman lying on his bed sound asleep. She was the innocent party— the bystander that would get hurt—and he had no idea how to protect her. The only thing he did know was that the longer he kept up this pretense of being her assistant instead of the heir to the QTR empire—the worse it was going to be when the truth finally won out—and it would. The truth always came to light—sometimes at the most inopportune times.

Continue reading
MISS WHITE AND THE SEVENTH HEIR
Jennifer Faye

Available next month
www.millsandboon.co.uk

LET'S TALK
Romance

For exclusive extracts, competitions
and special offers, find us online:

f facebook.com/millsandboon

🅞 @millsandboonuk

🐦 @millsandboon

Or get in touch on 0844 844 1351*

For all the latest titles coming soon, visit
millsandboon.co.uk/nextmonth